The Saloon Owner's Unwelcome Winter Bride

Cheryl Wright

Copyright

THE SALOON OWNER'S UNWELCOME WINTER BRIDE
(Unwelcome Brides Series – Book Seven)

Copyright ©2025 by Cheryl Wright

Small Town Romance Publications

Dedication

To Margaret Tanner, my very dear friend and fellow author, for her enduring encouragement and friendship.

To Alan, my husband of over fifty years, who has been a relentless supporter of my writing and dreams for many years.

To You, my wonderful readers, who encourage me to continue writing these stories. It is such a joy knowing so many of you enjoy reading my stories as much as I love writing them for you.

Table of Contents

Chapter One..6

Chapter Two..11

Chapter Three...18

Chapter Four..26

Chapter Five..32

Chapter Six...40

Chapter Seven...46

Chapter Eight...52

Chapter Nine..58

Chapter Ten...64

Chapter Eleven..70

Chapter Twelve..76

Chapter Thirteen..82

Chapter Fourteen..88

Chapter Fifteen...94

Chapter Sixteen..101

Chapter Seventeen..107

Chapter Eighteen...112

Chapter Nineteen...117

Chapter Twenty...124

Chapter Twenty-One...129

Chapter Twenty-Two 135

Chapter Twenty-Three 140

Epilogue 148

From the Author 152

About the Author 153

Links 154

Chapter One

Esther Beaufort opened her eyes, only to discover she was lying on a strange bed.

As she tried to sit up, her head spun. Glancing about the room, Esther had no idea where she was. What she did know was she'd been drugged. The last thing she recalled was walking home from her job at the local diner. She was confronted by two men who wrestled her to the ground.

After that terrifying recollection, there was nothing.

Every day she walked home that same way, cutting through the laneway. Never before had she encountered a problem. Except, this time she'd worked later than normal. It was bordering on darkness. In hindsight, it wasn't the brightest idea she'd ever had.

Now she had to contend with…whatever this was.

She slowly brought herself upright. This time she felt a little more stable. Waiting until she felt able, Esther eventually stood. She was barefooted, and what was she wearing? Glancing down at herself, Esther was horrified. The gown she wore revealed far more of her womanly assets than any man, other than a husband, had a right to see.

Still unsteady on her feet, she carefully walked to the dresser on the other side of the room, and sat down. Esther peered into the mirror attached to the dresser. Her own face was barely recognizable. It was plastered with bright red lipstick, red rouge on her cheeks, and color on her eyelids.

Her heart thudded. She would never use such garish items.

Only now did she have a better view of what she was wearing. Who had taken her clothes, the ones that portrayed her modesty? An even worse question came to mind – who had dressed her in this more than a little revealing outfit?

Esther stared angrily at the disturbing image. This was not the Esther Beaufort she knew. This woman looked like a whore.

Her heart rate increased and her head pounded as reality set in. She had been drugged, kidnapped, and brought here to work as a whore.

Searching through the dresser drawers, Esther found her clothes – ripped to shreds. Whoever stole her off the street was sending her a message. She was here, and now belonged to him. He knew she wouldn't be seen dead on the streets wearing this obscene outfit.

Esther had news for him. She wasn't waiting around to be violated. It was then she noticed movement over her shoulder. Until that moment, Esther believed she was alone. But in a terrible twist of fate, she now understood she wasn't. Her heart thudded as a man sat across the other side of the room. An evil smile came to his lips. "You're awake," he said, a lecherous grin now crossed his face. "I will be your first, my dear," he said, then began to stand.

Barefoot or not, Esther had no intention of waiting around.

~*~

Esther moved far more quickly than she thought possible, knocking the vile creature over in her wake. She'd taken him by surprise, that much was clear.

Did he expect her to simply comply with his wishes? He may have drugged her with evil intent, but Esther was having none of it. She had no time to think, and ran as far as her short legs would take her.

Not contemplating the scenario where he caught up with her in record time, Esther ran like Satan himself was on her tail. In truth, he was Satan. Anyone who believed it was acceptable to kidnap and drug women had to be in cahoots with the devil. There was no other explanation.

Flinging the door open, she ran out onto the carpeted balcony. It was quiet, no one was around except Esther and the wicked man chasing her. She could hear him coming but didn't look back. That would take too much energy. Instead she focused on getting away from this sinful place. She shuddered as she ran down the wide stairs.

She heard the tinker of glass as she dashed past the bar, and prayed the barman situated there did not react quickly enough to snatch her before she got away. A heavy wooden door stood between Esther and freedom, and her worst fear was it would be locked. Her heart fluttered in panic. What if she couldn't escape? Her life as she knew it would be over. Esther couldn't face the reality of the life he had planned for her.

She grasped the door handle with both hands and pulled. Surprisingly, the door opened. She rushed out onto the street, her pursuer not far behind. "You will regret this," he shouted as she continued to run.

Glancing about, Esther noticed the stagecoach not far up the road. It was pulling out onto the road. She ran through the snow and sludge, and almost fell to the ground. Ignoring the pain in her bare feet, she continued to run. She was desperate to get away, and steadied herself before she fell.

She had no idea where the stagecoach was headed, and neither did she care. Esther reached out, and to her great surprise, managed to get hold of something on the stagecoach. She hung on for dear life, and had no intention of letting go. Finally, she managed to pull herself up.

As the speed of the stagecoach increased, Esther scrambled to find a safe place where she couldn't fall. It would do her no good to escape the brothel, only to fall to her death in the process.

Chapter Two

Parker Gerard both heard and felt the thud as the stagecoach left Johnsonville. Out of the corner of his eye, he'd seen a young woman scramble onto the back of the coach. Surely he was mistaken?

Any other time he would ask the driver to stop. Only this time he was being more cautious. As he stared out the window, looking past the stagecoach, was a man. Parker knew this man, but only by reputation.

If he wasn't mistaken, he owned the largest brothel in the entire county. Taking women against their will was the way he built his business. Parker felt ill at the mere thought of it. What kind of person treated women in this way?

The answer was clear – someone with no scruples whatsoever. For a man to do this, he couldn't be called a man. He should be jailed. Unfortunately, Parker was not in a position to do anything about it. Not while he was on the stagecoach.

He shuddered. Parker knew he had to do something. Anything. The woman needed rescuing.

He could hear her wriggling about. Unless she managed to get to the top of the coach, her life was in peril. He glanced out the window again. This time looking up. There was nothing to see there, which filled him with terror.

Had she fallen to her death? His heart rate increased. He might not know the woman, but he still worried for her. Glancing back the way they came, Parker checked to ensure they weren't being followed.

So far they were alone. It didn't mean they could be complacent. "Ma'am," he called, his head out of the window. "Are you alright?" He reached out, trying to locate her, but the woman didn't respond. Nor was he able to reach her.

It wouldn't be long and they'd arrive at a small town. Mostly, the stagecoach didn't stop there. The town was so small, there were rarely passengers to collect or drop off. "Driver," Parker called to no avail. "Bert!" This time he shouted. "We need to stop at the next town." To his surprise, the closer they got, the slower the stagecoach moved. Until finally, they pulled up.

The driver, Bert, climbed down and opened the door. "What is the urgency?" he demanded, clearly annoyed at the unscheduled stop.

"There's a woman up there," he whispered, pointing to the roof.

The driver glared at him. "Don't be stupid. If anyone was on this stagecoach, I'd know about it. Besides, you are the only passenger today." He turned and began to climb up again.

"Humor me," Parker said. He was a regular on this line, and an esteemed customer. He hoped it would be enough for Bert to give in to his demands.

Parker scrambled out of the coach so quickly, it gave Bert no choice. Parker immediately went to the back, to the trunk where luggage was stored. And just as he'd predicted, there she was, holding on for dear life. "It's safe," Parker said, his arms outstretched. "Let me help you down."

She shook her head, and his heart sank. He should have known she would not be trusting of a stranger. Especially strange men. "I promise, I will not harm you," he said gently.

"Please…don't make me go back there," she said quietly, her voice wavering with each word.

"Never!" he said with conviction. "My intention is to ensure your safety. Right now, you are not safe." He motioned for her to let go so he could help her down. "I'll catch you and keep you safe, I promise," he said with far more confidence than he felt. "I never break my promises."

To his surprise, the woman let go, and slid down the trunk, into his waiting arms.

Breathing a sigh of relief, Parker gazed into the face of the woman. Her face was covered in gaudy make up. He was certain it was not placed there with her permission. Much like the revealing clothes she wore.

As he held her in his arms, Parker knew he had to do something to help her. What that was, he wasn't sure. He was about to place her on the ground when he noticed her bare feet. "Where are your boots?" he asked gently.

Tears swam in her eyes. "I don't know. I found my clothes, but they were shredded and useless. My boots were not with them."

Parker's head spun. He'd heard nothing but terrible things about the brothel owner, but didn't expect anything like this. "It's alright," he whispered. "I will assist you." Instead of placing her on the rough ground as he'd planned, Parker instead, carried her to the stagecoach and placed her inside. He removed his jacket, and helped her into it.

The driver stared at him. "Can we go now?" Bert's eyes bore into him, but Parker didn't care. His only concern was keeping this woman safe.

Parker thought about it for a moment. "Not quite yet," he said, then hurried into the stage office. There he bought a ticket for his new companion, then went into the men's room momentarily, returning with a dampened cloth. "Now we can leave," he said, when he returned. Then climbed into the stagecoach, sitting near to the woman. Not too close though. She'd been through enough and didn't need the grief.

As she sat quietly, Parker wasn't sure how to approach the subject. In the end, he just came out and said it. "I brought something to clean that trash off your face," he said gently, wondering if he could have said it any better. Gentler. She didn't flinch, nor did she refuse.

He heard her sigh. "Thank you. I…I can't believe what they did to me." Tears ran down her face, and Parker wasn't sure what he should do. Ignore the tears and clean her face of make up? Or comment on how much better her tears would make her feel?

Instead, he handed her the dampened cloth. It was then he realized he didn't know her name. He sat patiently, waiting for her to finish. Little did he know she was desperate to clean her face. So much so, she wiped it over and over again.

Until Parker put his hand over hers to stop the woman damaging her skin. She didn't say a word, instead her blue eyes studied him. "What is your name?" he asked, his voice almost a whisper.

She studied him some more, and Parker completely understood the reason. He was no one to her. He might have helped her, but apart from that, she didn't know him. Parker realized then, she could think he was working with the brothel owner. He took the soiled cloth from her hands. Most of the make up was gone. He reached out to expel the remaining make up, but she pulled back. She had a long road ahead. He had no doubt about that.

"Esther," she whispered. "Esther Beaufort."

He had no reason to believe she wasn't telling the truth. "Where are you from, Esther. We need to let your family know you are safe."

She shook her head. "If I have family, I don't know who they are." She shook her head again. "They drugged me, and I…can't think straight. She wrung her hands in her lap. Pink flooded her cheeks, which was probably a good thing. Until that moment she was deathly pale.

Her words explained a lot. Unscrupulous brothel owners targeted women like this. Those who had no one looking out for them. No one to notice they were missing.

"Oh," she suddenly said. "I think I live in Helena."

Helena? They were miles from there. No family, and they'd taken her quite a distance from home. Esther was perfect for criminals like this. Except, now her face was no longer painted, he could see she wasn't a young woman. Esther had to be late thirties. Maybe even a little older? "You can't go back there. Not alone anyway," he said. "The same thing could happen again." The shocked look on her face surprised him. It was common sense. On the other hand, she seemed to believe she was drugged, which meant it was probably still in her system, fogging up her mind.

Parker knew he had to get her to a doctor, and report her kidnapping to the sheriff. But not here. They were far too close to where he first saw her.

In that moment, Parker knew he had to take her home with him. What she would think about that, he dared not ponder.

Chapter Three

Esther tried to keep her eyes open, but the constant rocking of the stagecoach lulled her into a deep sleep. The man sitting next to her, he was her savior. Yet, she didn't know his name. She needed to ask. Right now though, she couldn't think straight. Maybe a short nap would help. She stopped fighting her body's urge to make her sleep, and soon drifted off.

What seemed a short time later, she awoke with a start, only to find her rescuer's hands holding her around the waist. Perhaps he wasn't the man he professed to be, after all.

"You almost fell off the seat," he said before she had a chance to open her mouth. "Better I hold you, than you land on the uncomfortable floor."

He was right and Esther knew it. "Thank you," she said warily, then glanced about.

Nodding, he helped her back onto the seat. "We'll arrive in just a few minutes," the stranger told her.

Esther's heart thudded. She had no idea where she was. Nor did she know where the man was transporting her. "What is your name?" she asked once she recalled she hadn't asked. "And where are you taking me?"

He offered her his hand, but she didn't take it. Would he understand her hesitation? Surely he couldn't blame her, not one iota. For all she knew he could be in cahoots with the man who'd had her kidnapped. He pulled his hand back and studied her. "Parker Gerard," he said. "I own…a business here in town."

Esther felt shock ripple through her. This man, albeit the one who rescued her, wanted to take her to a place he owned? A place she knew nothing about? Sweat formed above her lip. Her first instinct was to run the moment the stagecoach stopped. Except she had nowhere to go. She could run to the sheriff's office, but what would she do after that? She needed a place to stay where she would be safe from further attempts to install her in the brothel.

She was no one's fool, and Esther knew if they managed to drag her back there again, she would never leave. She would again be drugged, but this time, the brothel owner would ensure she never stepped outside again.

The thought was sobering. And downright terrifying.

"What business?" she asked once her mind cleared of the frightening thoughts regarding her future.

Parker studied her closely, for what seemed forever. "I own the saloon here in Silvercrest," he said, his voice strong and steady.

Esther detected something in his voice. Was that guilt? It was then his words sank in. "Saloon? I…"

"It is not that kind of establishment," he said firmly. "I do not run a brothel, nor will I ever run one." He ran a hand through his hair, and Esther could sense his frustration. "I can provide you with a safe haven until you're ready to leave. Whenever that might be."

A safe haven. It sounded like something she should accept without hesitation. After recent events, she was far more wary than she'd ever been. Esther wasn't sure how she should respond. Instead, she nodded and glanced down at her entwined hands as they sat frozen on her lap.

"Silvercrest," the driver called as he brought the stagecoach to a stop. After he'd climbed down, he opened the door, putting the steps in place.

"Thanks, Bert," Parker said, then alighted the coach, then helped Esther down the few steps. She still wore his jacket, and attempted to hand it back to him. "Not here," he said. "Let's get you settled back at the saloon, then we can think about your attire."

"But…" she began, not knowing how to repay this stranger for all the help he'd given her.

He'd held her hands as she moved down the few steps. Esther didn't complain. The way his touch made her feel, Esther already knew she was in trouble. She told herself it was merely a reaction to the man who had saved her from a fate worse than death.

A shiver went down her spine as he gazed at her. "You alright?" he asked, a frown on his face.

What could she say? His touch affected her in the strangest of ways? Admitting it would never do. "I'm fine," she said instead, and breathed a sigh of relief at being on solid ground again.

"Good," he said. "Once I have my luggage, we can go. It's not far."

Except she had to walk through the town in this horrible outfit. At least the worst of it was covered by Parker's jacket. She was thoroughly grateful to him for providing her with the damp cloth to clean her face. Without a mirror, she had no idea how much, if any of the make up was still there.

"There's a short cut," he said as they moved away from the stage office after collecting his meagre luggage. A small overnight bag was all he'd needed for his short trip to Johnsonville.

Esther gasped. A short cut? Like the one she'd taken to get home that night? The one that left her wide open to be kidnapped, drugged, and set up to become a whore? "I…" She closed her eyes against the memory. Knowing she would not cope going down a back alley or even a narrow street, had her heart pounding. Esther had never been afraid before. Not in her entire life. At least, not like this.

Parker studied her, but Esther couldn't work out why. She felt light-headed. Most likely from the terror she felt by simply hearing those words – short cut. She heard a thud and then Parker had his hands on her. Without warning, Esther sensed she was about to faint.

The moment she awoke, Esther studied her surroundings. She had no idea where she was. Nor did she know who'd brought her here. Had she been recaptured and returned to the brothel? Her heart sank.

Before she had a chance to sit up, or even to attempt to escape, someone squeezed her hand. "Ah, you're awake." The voice was unfamiliar to her, but Esther sensed she was safe. "I am Doctor Billings, but everyone calls me Doc." He chuckled, enticing Esther to glance up at his circular face. He wasn't old, but nor was he young. His face was attractive in its own way. But most importantly, it was a face that made you want to trust him.

"How? Where?" She couldn't think straight, and it showed.

Doc patted her hand. "You fainted. Lucky for you, Parker carried you here. He's a good man. A decent man." On those last words, Doc nodded. "You are still suffering from the effects of the drugs you were given. It appears you haven't eaten for a number of days either. That would be due to being drugged and sleeping for several days."

Parker must have told him. There was no other way Doc would know her history. She wasn't sure whether to thank Parker for passing on the information, or be mad at him for the same reason. The more she thought about it, the more she realized Parker was trying to help her. Without that information, Doc wouldn't be able to treat her appropriately. "You can stay here a little longer, or you can go home now. It depends on how you feel."

Go home? She couldn't go home for fear of her safety. Esther had no home here, so was unsure what she would do. Her reticule and any money she had on her was gone. Thankfully, it wasn't much – she only ever carried a small amount with her, and the rest went straight into the bank.

"I'm taking her back to the saloon. She'll be safe there." Parker's voice seemed a long way off. When he squeezed her hand, Esther knew he was close by. She wasn't sure why everyone was being so kind to her. They didn't know her, and she had no way to repay them.

Doc Billings voice seemed to boom above her. "Good. She'll need to rest for a few days. Don't you go putting her to work."

His last sentence had Esther panicking. Put her to work? Did that mean…? Her entire body stiffened, and almost immediately, Parker was standing over her.

"Oh my gosh," Doc Billings said. "I didn't mean it to come out that way. Parker runs a clean business. His business has a kitchen and front end staff. That's all I meant." He turned to face the saloon owner, and then her. "I'm sorry," he said. "I truly am."

Esther breathed a massive sigh of relief. She should have known better. Parker had been nothing but kind to her. There were men who used kindness as a way to fool women into doing what they wanted, but Parker wasn't like that. She was reminded of that at every turn.

Doc Billings helped her to sit up, then stood next to her. "Any dizziness? Light-headedness?"

"None," she said, which wasn't totally true. Her head spun, but so little Esther was convinced it wouldn't be an issue.

As though Doc saw through her façade, he demanded she sit there for a few minutes before leaving. Esther was about to protest, but Parker stepped forward and stood right there with her. As if guarding her. Protecting Esther from herself. It was then she wondered why she was in such a rush to leave.

Chapter Four

"Home sweet home," Parker said as they entered the saloon via a back entrance. The last thing he wanted was to have Esther paraded through the front entrance. Especially dressed the way she was. Pulling a set of keys from his pocket, Parker paused momentarily before unlocking the door. He led her up the stairs, to the top level, and unlocked a second door.

He waited for her protest, but none came. He concluded Esther was simply glad to be off the streets and away from prying eyes. "Take a seat," he said, motioning for her to sit on one of the comfortable chairs. "I'll take my luggage into the bedroom, and be back shortly." He watched as she grimaced, but wasn't sure why she did. Until he watched her carefully.

Esther was in fight or flight mode. She was ready to run. Where to, he had no idea, but her whole demeanor told him she had misunderstood his intentions. "There's a guest bedroom," he said gently. "Let me take you there." He reached out and helped Esther to her feet.

As they reached the room, she appeared to relax somewhat. Still, she didn't let down her guard. He knew when someone was on the edge, and recognized that in Esther. He walked over to the window and opened it slightly. "This room has been closed up for a very long time," he said. "I don't often have visitors." He watched as she relaxed a little more.

Esther glanced about the room. It was fairly large, but not as big as the master bedroom. The owner's suite was already built when Parker bought the saloon. That was some years ago now. This area was not available to customers, only Parker, and now Esther.

"There is a locked door at the bottom of the stairs, on the restaurant side," he said. "It prevents customers from finding their way up here. It is not designed to keep anyone in. It was designed to keep unauthorized people out."

He watched as her eyes roamed the room. She stood looking all forlorn, and Parker wasn't certain how to help her further. Then it occurred to her. "I'll get the mercantile owner's wife over here. She can outfit you. Until that happens, I'm sure a hot bath would help?"

Her eyes opened wide, then a smile came to Esther's face. "That would be nice," she said quietly. "Except I have no money for clothes."

"Money is not an issue. We'll sort something out down the track if it makes you happy. On my part, you owe me nothing." Parker's heart fluttered as he said the words, and he had no idea why.

Esther gave him the strangest look, then opened her mouth to speak. Then closed it again. She sat down on the edge of the bed that had barely been used since he arrived a few years earlier. "I owe you everything," she whispered. "Without you, I would be a whore by now." Tears swam in her eyes, until they finally ran down her pale cheeks. It was the first time she'd let herself cry, and Parker was glad to see her finally letting her emotions out.

It couldn't have been easy for her. None of it could.

He wanted to hold her. To tell Esther it would all be alright. Except he couldn't promise her anything. If the brothel owner got so much as a whiff of where she was located, Esther would be in grave danger once again.

Before he could stop himself, Parker went to her side and wrapped Esther in his arms. She cried silently against his chest, and he imagined this was exactly where she was meant to be. Right here in his arms. Except it was a ridiculous thought. He had merely saved her from a fate worse than death, and brought her to his home where she would be safe.

So why did he feel so comfortable and content? The last thing Parker wanted was a relationship. This had to stop – he needed to push her away and go about his business.

He couldn't bring himself to do it.

Instead, Esther did it for him. "We…I shouldn't be doing this," she said quietly, her voice so low he almost missed it.

Parker's arms dropped away, and he felt hollow. Why, he had no idea. They'd known each other for a couple of hours at most. All he could think was he felt responsible for her. Esther needed someone to take care of her. To ensure her safety, and he was ready to take on the responsibility, even though it wasn't his place to do so.

Frankly, he had no choice. She was completely alone in the world, or at least she thought she was. She was also in a strange town. Which begged the question. "Why were you out so late that night?" The moment he asked the question, Parker knew he'd done the wrong thing. "My apologies. None of this was your fault. You have every right to go out at a time of your choosing."

Esther stared at him with those piercing blue eyes. Then she shook her head. Did that mean she couldn't believe he'd asked such a thing? "I was working late. Far later than usual." She brushed her disheveled hair back off her face. "I am…was…a cook at the diner. We had a private engagement, so I left late."

Fury built inside Parker. "You were left to walk home alone? In the dark? Such behavior is inexcusable," he ground out. His mind went in all directions. What if the diner owner was in cahoots with the brothel owner? Parker shook himself mentally. The towns were over an hour apart. Surely that scenario was not feasible? "Let me show you the bathroom," he said, trying to rid himself of the ridiculous thoughts going through his mind. "You will find any toiletries you may require in the cupboard. Towels can be found there, too." He wanted his guest to be happy and comfortable. Most of all, he wanted her to feel safe.

To be safe.

While the bath water ran, Parker fetched the luxurious robe he kept for visitors. "Put this on after your bath. I'll arrange for the mercantile owner's wife to come once you're done." He immediately saw a frown cross Esther's face. "No hurry. I have things to do first, so take your time." Opening the cupboard doors, he retrieved a white fluffy towel, along with a number of toiletries. "Bubbles," he said, handing over a large bottle of bubbles made specifically for this purpose. "I keep it for visitors."

He then left the room, pulling the door closed. "Don't forget to lock the door," he shouted from the other side. Parker worried about his unexpected visitor. It took little for her to become panicked, but he understood the reasons completely.

Standing next to the door, he waited until he heard the click of the lock. Then he relaxed. While Esther enjoyed a leisurely bath, he had chores to do. The most important one was to arrange clothes and other necessary items for Esther. For now, enough to rid her of the awful get up designed for women of the night. After that, who knew? Parker had no idea how long his visitor would be staying, but most importantly, however long it took, he wanted her to be kept away from the notorious brothel owner.

Chapter Five

Esther settled down into the hot bath, and immediately felt better. Surrounded by fragrant bubbles, it felt like she was living a life of luxury. In reality, she was fleeing for her life. Parker had got her this far, and hidden her away. For how much longer could he do that?

Yes, he had this exclusive suite, hidden away from the saloon and presumably the rest of the town. That didn't mean he could keep her existence hidden indefinitely. Nor would he want to. He seemed a decent man. His actions so far had proven it. Still, she needed to be vigilant. Esther worried whether Parker was keeping her hidden to allow the brothel owner to come and collect her.

She shook herself mentally. Parker didn't seem the type. If his plan had been to hand her back over to the evil man, wouldn't he have already done so? A shiver went down her spine. If she hadn't run for her life, where would she be right now?

Esther didn't want to know the answer to the question. It was not worth thinking about.

Despite having already washed her face several times, she lifted the water filled face cloth, and wiped at her face again. It surely had to be completely clean now? Instead of worrying about her face, which could be easily checked once she was out of the bath, she focused on her hair instead. Washing it with the toiletries Parker had given her, Esther knew she had never felt so pampered. He didn't come across that way, but the man had to be rich. Didn't he?

He'd already told her money was not an issue, but he could have been trying to appease her. If only she had access to her bank account. Except the downside of doing so, meant she was traceable.

As she washed the filth out of her hair, Esther began to feel normal again. Although she wasn't sure what was normal anymore. Her usual routine was going to work each day, and coming home to her cozy cottage where she felt safe.

Parker told Esther she could never return home and be safe. At the time, she didn't agree. Now she'd had time to think it through, she knew he was right.

The tap on the bathroom door alerted Esther she had probably dallied far too long. "Esther?" Parker's voice was quiet, and barely loud enough for her to hear. "Ruby, the mercantile owner's wife, will be here shortly. Don't rush, though. Take your time."

It was then Esther realized she'd been in the water far too long. She stared at her hands. They were wrinkled and overly soft. The water, when she checked, felt lukewarm. Both were a clear indication she'd lost track of time.

"I'm coming," she called back, and hurried to stand, almost slipping. If she fell and needed assistance, she was certain Parker would break the door down if necessary. And see her in all her naked glory.

That would never do.

As much as Esther appreciated everything Parker had done for her, and was still doing, she had no intention of letting her rescuer see her naked.

Reaching for the towel, Esther pondered her situation. Not through any fault of her own, she'd been kidnapped and drugged. All for the sole purpose of making money for the most sinful person she'd ever encountered.

Her heart pounded at the thought. Had she not made the decision to run, Esther knew exactly where she would be now – flat on her back in that horrible place. Her new home. No longer would she be free to do whatever she pleased, and no decent man would want anything to do with her.

It was enough to bring tears to her eyes, but Esther fought them back. Parker Gerard had put himself in danger to help her. She would be forever grateful to him for his unexpected act of kindness.

Esther pulled on her undergarments, as soiled as they may be. She was always a stickler for hygiene, and doing this made her skin crawl. What choice did she have? She pulled on the soft and luxurious robe, and wrapped it around herself. Never had she felt such luxury against her delicate skin. Parker certainly knew how to look after his guests.

After drying her hair, Esther brushed it as quickly as was feasible.

She took a deep breath, and counted slowly to ten. Now she felt ready to face Parker and the mercantile owner's wife.

The moment she opened the bathroom door, Esther felt two sets of eyes focus on her. A shiver ran down her spine as she prepared for what was to come.

Parker stood, and stepped toward her. "Esther," he said gently. "This is Ruby from the mercantile. She will get you set up with whatever you need."

Esther knew she could never repay Parker for all his kindness and generosity. At least not until she had access to her money again. "I…" She wasn't sure what to say. Instead, she reached over and shook the other woman's hand.

Ruby was a big lady, rotund and more than a little friendly, as Esther discovered quickly. "I'm so pleased to meet you," she said excitedly, pulling Esther into a tight hug. "What a pity your luggage was stolen."

Esther glanced across at Parker. He'd obviously made up a story to protect her. Esther truly appreciated it. "Thank you. It was devastating. My reticule was stolen, too," she said. It wasn't a lie – the brothel owner had confiscated it to keep her from leaving. Except his plan didn't work.

"I suggest we go into the guest bedroom." She leaned in to Esther and whispered. "We have more privacy there."

The moment they entered the guest room, Esther believed they'd taken a wrong turn. There were clothes strewn all over the bed. There were piles of various gowns, skirts, and blouses. Not to mention the unmentionables. She hoped Parker hadn't seen those.

Esther felt the heat rise up her face at the mere thought of it.

Ruby turned and closed the door against the only male present. The one who decided this was necessary. "Parker told me to fit you out properly for a week at least. I've bought a selection of clothes that I believe will interest you." Ruby stood back and studied Esther. "I know this is rather intrusive, but I need to see you without the robe." Esther frowned. "To work out your sizing, my dear," Ruby told her.

Esther reluctantly complied, but didn't have to be happy about it. Especially knowing her undergarments were not in the best state.

Ruby studied her figure for only moments, then turned to the piles of clothes on the bed. She held up a beautiful gown that Esther could only dream about. "That is way too expensive," Esther protested.

Waving a hand in front of herself, Ruby scoffed. "Parker has authorized me to outfit you, no matter the cost. This is just one gown. There are several more to choose from." Ruby put the gown aside.

Esther knew what she was doing – Ruby was appeasing her, for now. She had no doubt the mercantile owner's wife would circle back to this particular gown when the time was right. "This one would suit you perfectly," Ruby said, holding up a different gown. One with a much lower price tag.

She then held it against Esther and suggested she check her reflection in the full length mirror. It did appear to suit her coloring, and Esther agreed to try it on. It fitted perfectly. Ruby put it aside by hanging it on the rail in the robe. It was as though a decision had been made for her. Had decisions been taken out of her hands? Esther wasn't sure. What she was certain about was Parker and Ruby both had her best interests at heart.

She truly appreciated it.

What seemed like an hour or more later, decisions were made about clothes, as well as undergarments, nightgowns and robes. She also had boots to wear, which was helpful when it was again safe to go outside.

She helped Ruby pack up what wasn't required, and offered to help carry them back to the store. She couldn't believe she'd already forgotten the precarious situation she found herself in. Both Parker and Ruby had made her feel right at home. In other circumstances, she and Ruby would probably become the best of friends. Right now though, she needed to lay low, and keep out of the public eye.

"Thank you, but no thank you, my dear," Ruby said gently. "Parker told me about your skin condition. It must be difficult not to be able to go outside for extended periods of time." She grabbed an armful of the clothes and headed outside. "I'll be back for more soon," she said over her shoulder.

Esther felt terrible. All the lies the lovely woman had been told. Meant to keep Esther safe. She felt sure if Ruby knew the truth, she would be forgiving. She came across as a caring and gentle soul. Someone who would look out for those in need.

Esther was pleased to have met Ruby, but sad they'd never have the opportunity to get to know each other better.

Chapter Six

Parker couldn't help but stare at the vision before him. Esther had been transformed from what the brothel owner perceived as his property, to the beauty she must always have been.

He couldn't comprehend how anyone could manipulate and control women like that. He found their way of living with themselves unfathomable. It was undeniably true; some men were devoid of conscience.

He was thankful he did not fall into that category. He was so far different, it was beyond belief.

"You look lovely," he told her, as Esther finally left the guest bedroom. Ruby was long gone, and taken the excess supplies back to the store. She had apologized for the large bill, but Parker was surprised it was so low.

Esther's cheeks turned a pretty shade of pink. It was better than the ghostly pale pallor she'd had earlier. "It's all too much," she said quietly. "I asked Ruby to take more back to the store, but she wouldn't."

He could see his guest was more than a little upset. "She was following my orders. For the record, it isn't too much. It's what I requested. Ruby's job was to work out exactly what you needed, and fit you for the right outfits."

"But it costs…"

She stopped the moment he put up a hand to halt her words. "It is what you need, and what I want to do. You are in a very tricky predicament. What would happen to you otherwise?"

Esther's head went down as she averted her eyes. They both knew his words were true. "Accept it for what it is – a gift from one friend to another." He motioned for her to sit down on one of the comfortable chairs. "I have ordered food. I'm starving. What about you?" It was clear she had to be hungry. There was no way to be certain, but Esther believed she was taken some days ago. If she was drugged, as she obviously was according to Doc Billings, she hadn't eaten for the same amount of time.

"I can cook," she said, her way of protesting, he was sure. She glanced about. "Where is the kitchen?"

He chuckled then. "Down the stairs and to the left. All my meals come from the saloon kitchen." His words left her looking deflated. Why was she feeling that way? Parker thought about it for a moment, then realized – she wanted to pay him back for his kindness. "My assistance is not reciprocal," he said firmly. "You owe me nothing."

"You don't have any kitchen facilities up here? Not even somewhere to make basic meals?" She sounded almost distraught, but he couldn't understand why.

"There is one, but it's tiny, and I have never used it." he told her as he sat down beside her and reached for her hand. Parker knew he had no right, but felt compelled. This poor woman had been downtrodden not only by her employer, but by complete strangers. Men who decided to force her into a soiled dove they could manipulate and control for their own financial gain.

The very thought left him horrified and nauseous. If men were allowed to pluck women off the street at their pleasure, and place them in brothels, the world would be a terrible place. No, this couldn't be allowed to continue.

Parker would have to think on this. The sheriff should be consulted, but tonight was not the time to discuss law enforcement's involvement with Esther. She was still shocked from her terrifying ordeal. He would give her time to recover.

~*~

Supper was delicious as it always was. He'd ordered chicken pot pie for Esther, in the hope her stomach would cope with a lighter meal. Parker offered to exchange it for steak, or anything else if she wished, but she flat out declined his offer.

He'd asked Antoine, his chef, to send a dessert that could be construed as indulgent. He wanted only the best for Esther. And that was exactly what he got.

Vanilla Blancmange, surrounded by seasonal berries, and a light sauce made with the same fruit. Clotted cream sat on the side of the plate. The dessert appeared delicious, and from experience, Parker knew it was a melt in your mouth dish.

Although Esther didn't eat all her food, after pushing it around her plate for a short time, she'd finally taken a bite. She'd glanced up at him and smiled. "This is good," she said. "Thank you for ordering something light for me."

She had eaten about half her meal, and Parker was happy with that. Doc Billings told him not push her until the drugs were out of her system. The last thing Parker wanted to do was make her even more unwell.

The moment she pushed her plate away, Parker reached for her hand. "I'm glad you managed to eat something. Even a little is better than nothing." She glanced down at their entwined hands but didn't pull hers away. Nor did she protest. "Doc said the drugs you were fed could have an effect on your stomach," he continued.

She flinched, and Parker regretted his statement. He wanted to make her feel better, not worse.

"I don't feel too bad," Esther told him. "A little nauseous, but not too much. Thank you for your concern," she added quietly.

She was still pale, but Parker decided not to say it out loud. Esther had enough to contend with. She didn't need to concern herself with her pallor. If he was still concerned in the morning, he'd arrange for Doc Billings to see her again.

His biggest concern right now was keeping her confined to his suite and away from prying eyes. He felt sure the brothel owner wouldn't come looking for Esther, but Parker couldn't be certain. Getting the sheriff involved would be the best idea. He would know what to do. Wouldn't he?

Parker shook himself mentally. *Concentrate on the issue at hand*, he told himself. And that was getting food into Esther. Even if it was very little, something was better than nothing.

She reached for her water, and took a couple of sips. Parker pushed the plate of blancmange toward her. She glanced down at it and smiled. "Your cook, he is very good," she said, taking a mouthful of the dessert. "This has to be the best blancmange I've ever had. Except for my own, of course." Esther laughed, her voice a mere tinkle, yet it set the nerves of his spine in motion. He could listen to her laughter all day. It lifted his heavy heart, yet he didn't know why.

It had been a very long time since he'd felt any emotion toward another person. What he really meant was a woman. Any woman. Not like this. He'd closed his heart to those who had the power to hurt or leave him.

This situation was different. Esther's life was in danger, and he had no option but to save her.

Chapter Seven

Esther was enjoying her time with Parker. As much as she could enjoy herself after being drugged and kidnapped.

In all aspects, he came across as a wonderful man. Someone who really cared. She'd not experienced this level of kindness for a very long time. Esther knew she shouldn't, but she was beginning to have feelings for Parker.

Shaking herself mentally, Esther decided to distance herself from the man sitting opposite her at the dining table. It was clear money was no object to him, but money was not everything. Real feelings, and real emotions interested her more. Whether Parker was capable of it, was a question she may never have answered.

Instead she would treat him as a friend. A good friend, nonetheless, who had her best interest at heart.

"This really is delicious," Esther said after letting the dessert linger in her mouth momentarily. It was the best way to get the full flavor. She glanced up at her host. "You're doing it all wrong," she told him.

Parker frowned.

"Here, let me," she said, taking the spoon out of his hand. As she scooped up some of the dessert, along with some berries, she fed him as though he was a child. "Do *not* swallow it," she demanded. "Not yet. Hold it in your mouth for ten seconds. Longer if you prefer."

He gazed at her, his confusion clear. Then his eyes opened wide.

"Now you can swallow it," she said, trying to stop herself from tittering. "It's good, right?"

Parker swallowed the delicate dessert, then gazed at her. "The flavor is completely different." She smiled, warmth filling her. "Where did you learn to do that?" he asked gently.

"When I did my chef training." She suddenly slapped a hand to her mouth. Esther knew she'd already given away too much about herself. Besides, Parker didn't need to know her life story. The truth was, he probably didn't want to know anything about her. After all, he'd planned for her to be here for a week, no more.

What she would do after that, Esther had no idea. She couldn't go back to Helena. Not to her home, and not to her job. Where she would end up, was anyone's guess.

She glanced up to find him staring at her. "You told me you were a cook," his eyes seemed to accuse as he studied her. "A chef is a whole different level of expertise."

What could she say? Parker was right, but jobs for chefs were hard to come by. Which was proven by the fact a chef was working here in the saloon. Most establishments of this nature, at least those Esther had come across, had terrible food. So bad, only the drunks would eat it.

"Your chef is excellent. The food is amazing. How did you snag someone so talented?" Except she already knew it was because of the lack of jobs in the area of cooking. Few diners existed, and most saloons had no care for the quality of food. Esther had been lucky to secure a job at the diner. Competition was fierce in Helena. There were several diners and cafés, not to mention a number of saloons.

She was offered a job, but only at cook's rates. It was a blow, but better than no job at all. She had supported herself for many years, and was lucky to have this job. Except now it was gone. Through no fault of her own, Esther could never return to her home.

Or the life she'd known.

"What are you thinking?" Parker's voice brought her back to reality.

"How lucky I've been until now," she whispered. "What…what happened has changed my entire life. I have to decide what to do now."

He shook his head. "There's plenty of time for that. Don't rush into anything. You have a place to stay for as long as you need it."

Esther stared at him. Did Parker really mean what he said? Or was it an empty promise? "You are too kind," she said, her voice a whisper. She had no idea why she was whispering. There was only her and Parker. No one else was there to overhear their conversations.

They both finished off their desserts, then Esther began packing up the soiled dishes. It was out of habit than anything else. "Leave those," Parker said firmly. "I have staff for that." He stood then, taking his coffee with him. "We'll retire to the sitting room. It's far more comfortable there."

She snatched up her mug of tea, and followed him. Parker was right – the sitting room chairs were thickly padded and luxurious. Esther had never seen such a richly furnished room. Or suite for that matter. Still, her assumption he was rich was unfounded, and could be completely untrue. Parker told her the suite came with the business. That didn't mean his business was thriving, although what she'd learned so far indicated she was correct.

"Sit down and relax," he told her once they were in the cozy room. He placed his coffee on a side table and went to the fireplace. It was burning well, and he threw some logs on the fire. It wasn't particularly cold in this room, but Esther was certain it would be, had the fire not been burning well.

"About your offer to stay," Esther said to his back, not certain how he would react. "You've done so much for me already."

Still crouched down at the fire, Parker turned to face her, a pained look on his face. He threw a few twigs into the center, then stood. "I can't force you to stay," he said gently, "but those men, the ones who kidnapped you? They are vicious. What they did to you? You weren't the first. They simply take what or who they want, consequences be damned."

His words came out as a snarl. It was as though this was personal. Except it couldn't be. Until today, neither knew the other even existed. Esther studied him. Their eyes met. They had a connection, but Esther couldn't understand why.

She strongly believed her situation was personal to him, but the reality was, she would probably never know the reason. Besides, it wasn't her business.

Parker stepped across the room, and returned to his chair. "I'm…sorry," he said. "I got carried away. I'm merely concerned for your safety and well-being."

Esther knew there was some reason for the sudden change in his demeanor, but had no idea what it might be. Nor was she ever likely to find out.

She'd crossed a line, and was truly sorry she had. Better to let sleeping dogs lie, as her mother always said.

Sipping her tea as she nodded, Esther had no intention of poking this sleeping dog any further. Especially since he was hell-bent on helping her.

Chapter Eight

Parker didn't know what had come over him. He was so fired up over Esther's situation, it had him on edge. He'd invited her to stay for a week, but knew it would likely be longer. Would he cope? The fact he'd all but snarled moments ago meant he was already affected by what happened to her.

It would never go away, that feeling of helplessness. As much as he wanted it to, he had no control over it. His only hope lie in helping Esther. If he aided her, ensured she was safe, would his feelings of guilt be appeased?

As much has he wanted it, Parker knew it was impossible. The guilt would always be there. Until the day he died. If he could help a survivor of those wretched men, all the better for everyone concerned.

His intense and penetrating thoughts were interrupted by a knock at the door. Esther visibly jumped, and ran into a corner of the room where she cowered.

This is what those evil men had done to her. They should be hung by the neck for their crimes. "It will be the kitchen staff, come for our tray," Parker told her gently as he squatted next to her. "No one else has access to this area."

Before opening the door, he led her back to where she'd sat comfortably only moments ago. His heart dissolved into fragments at the intense pain she felt. Her anguish became his. It seemed ridiculous after all this time, but the pain never went away. Nor did it lessen.

He opened the door to find his chef standing there. "Good evening, Parker," he said. "I hope the meal was to your liking. And that of your guest."

Parker couldn't help but grin. This entire exercise was to find out who he was entertaining. Who he'd ordered an exquisite dessert for. "Good evening, Antoine. The food was amazing as always." Parker began to turn away, then suddenly turned back. "Did you know if you hold the blancmange in your mouth for even ten seconds…" He stopped at the grin on his brother-in-law's face.

"Exactly who do you have in there?" Antoine asked, his curiosity peaked.

Parker leaned in closer and whispered. "I'm not sure she's ready to see anyone. However," he said conspiratorially, "she is a trained chef."

Antoine's eyebrows lifted. "Ah. This could be interesting," he said, then pushed his way inside the suite to collect the tray of dishes. "I shall leave you alone to your chef," he said, his amusement clear.

If only he knew, Parker thought, but right now was not the time to divulge anything more. No matter this man was family. As much as he knew Antoine would commiserate with both Esther and himself, Parker didn't want to share Esther's story at this point.

Nor would he. Not without her permission. None of this was her fault, and Antoine knew that better than anyone.

Antoine whistled as he gathered up the dishes, but suddenly stopped and turned to face Parker. "She didn't like the food?" he asked, a pained look on his face.

Parker's hand went to the other man's shoulder. "She…my visitor…is ill. Perhaps tomorrow she will feel a little better."

A frown appeared on Antoine's face. Now he understood and was not offended. "Yes, perhaps tomorrow she will feel better. Something light for breakfast, perhaps?" He rubbed a hand across his chin. "Scrabbled eggs for the lady? Light and fluffy as only Antoine can do."

Parker chuckled. Antoine was an excellent chef, a French chef. For some reason it gave him an elevated sense of importance. Granted there were few French chefs in this county, let alone the country, so he was an anomaly. *I trained under the best genuine French chefs*, he reminded Parker often.

Parker had rolled his eyes more times than he could count at the words, despite them being said in jest. "That sounds good," Parker said. "I'm sure E…she will appreciate it." It would never do to let slip any details about his visitor. He was working under the assumption the brothel owner would come after his prize. Parker knew more than likely it was true. He would not tell Esther under any circumstances. It was better she didn't know, than to spend every waking moment terrorized by the thought.

Closing the door behind his chef, Parker knew Antoine would not repeat any of their conversation. He was a pillar of society, and a wonderful man. Someone Parker could always rely on. Indeed, they leaned on each other when necessary, and had done so many times over the past years.

When he returned to the sitting room, Esther was right where he'd left her. In the luxurious chair – the one closest to the fire. He knew from experience being this close to the burning embers had an effect on a person's mood. Parker had been through a number of very dark days. He hadn't experienced the danger Esther was in now, or had been placed in, but he still knew the warmth of the fire could help her through it.

"My chef said he would make fluffy and light scrambled eggs for your breakfast," he said.

Her head shot up and she paled. "You told him about me?" Her concern was clearly visible on her face. "I…have to go. Now." She stood then, and Parker hurried to reassure her.

"He only knows I have a visitor. Someone who is ill and is eating light." He squatted in front of her, and held both her hands in his. "He doesn't even know your name, why you're here, or any other details."

He heard her sigh of relief, and was relieved himself. Parker had not meant to frighten or worry her, but had managed to do both. Color returned to her face. "Would you like another cup of tea?" he asked. "I can order it from the kitchen." He laughed then, and was pleased to see Esther smile.

"I need to see this kitchen of yours," she said, then stood.

Parker worried she would want to cook for them both, but couldn't deny such a simple request. He took her by the hand and led his guest to the tiny room. "You will be quite disappointed, I'm certain," he said.

When they entered the small room, Esther smiled. "This is perfect," she said, then began to open cupboards.

Chapter Nine

Esther glanced about the kitchen. Parker was right – it wasn't very big at all. However, it was large enough if she wanted to do some baking. There wasn't a lot to be happy about lately, but this discovery filled her heart with joy.

As much as Parker said he did not expect anything in return, Esther knew she would feel much better if she could do something, anything, to show her appreciation.

The oven was not the most modern, but was useable. It was, of course, far smaller than any oven she'd baked in before. Even her cottage kitchen was better than this one. She was resourceful, and could make it work.

Upon opening the cupboards, apart from a scant supply of crockery, her heart sank. Most of the cupboards were empty. "Is there a pantry?" she asked. Glancing about she couldn't see one.

"There's a small one," Parker said, and led her to it. "There are no supplies. I've relied on the saloon kitchen since the day I took over," he told her. "It was meant to be temporary, but I guess I got used to Antoine's excellent cooking." He grinned, and Esther couldn't be mad at him.

She thought for a minute before speaking again. "If I give you a list of requirements…"

"You don't have to cook," he said quickly, interrupting her.

Esther worried her bottom lip. It was a bad habit she had when she was worried about something. "I know that," she said firmly. "I want to do it." She leaned conspiratorially into him and whispered. "I. Am. Bored."

The shocked look on his face told Esther he had absolutely no idea it was the case. She waved a hand in front of herself. "It doesn't matter," she said, trying to keep the disappointment out of her voice.

Parker frowned. "Clearly, it does matter." He reached into one of the kitchen drawers and pulled out a notepad and pencil. "You can list your requirements here," he said, and handed them to her. "What did you want to make anyway?"

"I…I'm not sure," she said, her voice wavering. "Maybe muffins or pound cake. A pie perhaps? No matter what it is, it will be something delicious. What is your favorite?"

He grinned then. "All contributions gratefully accepted," he said, then chuckled.

Esther already enjoyed Parker's company, but a shiver went down her spine when he laughed. His lopsided grin already sent warmth coursing through her body, and it simply wouldn't do.

Esther knew she was in trouble, but also knew she had no choice but to stay here with Parker until the danger was over.

~*~

She had tossed and turned most of the night. As a result, she was exhausted. Not that Esther was surprised. After being abducted by strangers, drugged and held captive, it was no wonder. To top it all off, the moment she fell asleep, nightmares insinuated themselves, and she awoke screaming.

She'd dreamed Parker had come into her room and sat on the side of the bed, holding her hand until she settled again. It had seemed so real at the time, but Esther knew it was only a dream. When she finally opened her eyes to daylight, there in the comfortable chair not far from the bed sat Parker. Sound asleep.

She now knew it wasn't a dream after all. He had sacrificed his own sleep to take care of her. Again. Was there no end to this man's kindness?

She quietly climbed out of bed, trying not to wake him. He must be extremely tired if he'd spent much of the night trying to console and comfort her.

Esther quietly snatched up some clothes and headed for the bathroom.

Breakfast was already arranged, so she couldn't do anything in that direction. Nor did she have food supplies. She could however, ensure the fire was burning well before he awoke. She could also fuel the oven and prepare it for when she did have ingredients to work with. Was it any wonder she was bored? This place was functional, but barely.

What did Parker do all day? He hadn't left her side since she arrived there.

At that moment it hit her. He wasn't normally in his suite during the day. He had an office downstairs – he'd told her about it the previous day. He oversaw his staff and the saloon, and only came upstairs to eat and sleep.

Not only had he sacrificed his time to help her, but his business could suffer as a result. It simply wouldn't do.

What she could do about it, Esther had no idea. She couldn't let his business fail because of her. It would be the worst outcome possible. Except she wasn't sure what she could do to stop it happening. Parker was stubborn as a mule, and would deny everything.

Not that she'd known him long, but it was clear he was *the* most stubborn man she'd ever met. Trying to change his mind would be like trying to move a boulder after a century in the desert.

She twisted her long hair, pulling it up, and securing it in place. Ensuring it would hold, she reached for the bathroom door.

Esther froze. Her heart pounded. Was someone out there? She opened the bathroom door slightly and listened. This time she clearly heard it – a knock at the door. She crept down the hallway and toward the sound.

She felt somewhat reassured knowing the suite was in a secured area, but was still hesitant. What if her abductors had discovered her hiding place? And broken into the saloon? They could have killed anyone and everyone downstairs to get to her.

Esther was lightheaded with concern. Had she put others in danger? It was the last thing she wanted.

Another knock at the door. Moving to the front door, she listened. Perhaps they would go away if she ignored them.

According to Parker, the suite was impenetrable.

Or…this could be the breakfast tray Parker had arranged.. If it was the breakfast tray, the chef would not have time to make fresh food simply because she didn't answer the door. "Who…who is it?" she asked, lowering her voice to make herself sound masculine. Except it was the worst impression of a male voice she'd ever heard.

"It's Antoine. Is that you, Parker? Are you sick, too? I have your breakfast."

Relief flooded her, and Esther opened the door. Only slightly at first, but the moment the tray of food came into view, she opened it wider.

A huge grin crossed the man's face. This had to be Parker's chef. The chef's hat was a dead giveaway. "Good morning," he said, his endearing French accent clear to her.

"Good morning," she said warily. "Parker is still asleep."

Antoine frowned. "That is not like him. Parker is normally an early riser. Did he catch your illness?"

"Illness?" At first she was confused, but then Esther understood. "Oh no," she said. "You misunderstand. My stomach is a little…vulnerable right now."

He continued to frown, but Esther didn't want to explain. Not to this stranger, not to the sheriff, and not to anyone. Unfortunately, she was fully aware she would have no choice.

Chapter Ten

Parker awoke with a start.

He heard voices. One was male, the other female. His heart pounded – who had Esther opened the door for? Now standing, he forced himself not to panic. To calm down, and allow his heart rate to slow.

Cautiously, slowly, he moved toward the dining room. The vision before him sent ripples of relief down his spine. "Good morning," he said, forcing a smile to his face. "I see you two have met."

Antoine grinned at him. "Not really," he said, then reached out a hand to Esther. "I am Antoine. Head chef of this establishment." He chuckled then.

"You're the only chef," Parker said firmly. "The other workers are kitchen hands."

Esther glanced from one man to the other. She seemed to be assessing the pair. "I'm Esther," she said quietly, then floundered.

Parker stepped closer. "Esther is a friend," he told Antoine.

The chef raised his eyebrows. "A chef friend. You're not planning to replace me, are you, Brother?" he asked, then laughed.

Now Esther appeared confused. "Brother?" she asked.

"In-law. Antoine is my brother-in-law. At least…" He abruptly stopped talking, and the moment he did, Parker knew he now had to explain himself.

"I must interrupt," Antoine told him. "Breakfast is going cold. Sit down, both of you." It was an order, not a request, and neither denied him. The chef took the time to present each of them with their meal, then served their hot beverages. "Now, eat up," he commanded.

"You always were bossy," Parker said with a grin. He watched as Esther studied the scrambled eggs Antoine had made especially for her. Two pieces of crispy bacon sat to the side, along with perfectly cooked toast. His own plate contained two eggs, each beautifully poached, balanced on two slices of toast. Again, cooked to perfection. Several slices of bacon and grilled tomatoes also graced the plate. "You've outdone yourself, my friend," Parker told him.

Esther took a mouthful of her food. She closed her eyes as she savored the flavors, as she had taught him the night before. "This is good. Excellent, in fact," she said.

Antoine's face lit up. "A woman who appreciates good food. This one is a keeper," he said. Parker knew he shouldn't be annoyed, Antoine had no idea of Esther's situation. He had no plan of telling him, either. "I will leave you both to it," he said, then strolled out of the suite, leaving them completely alone.

"He seems nice," Esther said, then took another mouthful of food. "He is certainly an excellent chef."

Parker wasn't sure what to make of that, but decided she was talking from the point of view of one chef to another. "His food is always excellent," he said. He studied her briefly. "Why did you open the door? Why didn't you come and get me?" He sounded a little annoyed, which wasn't his intention at all.

She glared at him, and Parker knew he deserved it. "I vetted him. Through the door." Then she went back to her food as though nothing untoward had happened. "Anyway, you told me only authorized people could get up here."

Opening his mouth to speak, Parker then snapped it shut. Now was not the time. Besides, he *had* assured her those without the necessary credentials had no access to the suite. Not under any circumstances. Instead, he lifted the fork to his mouth. He let the flavor explode in his mouth before swallowing. Already Esther's influence had him changing his ways. Instead of gulping down his food, he now tasted every bite.

He was certain it had to be a good thing. Parker suffered greatly from indigestion, and perhaps this new way of eating may remedy it. Or perhaps, as he'd always believed, his overwhelming sense of guilt was the reason for his discomfort.

"Today," Esther said, waving her fork through the air, "I will write a shopping list. What should I make first? Muffins? Pie? Cookies?"

Her face lit up and Parker couldn't deny her the joy of doing something she loved. "Make your list whenever you are ready. More likely than not, Antoine will have the supplies in his kitchen."

Suddenly her face dropped. "Oh, Antoine. Will he be offended if I bake for you?"

Was this some sort of chef code? Not delving into each other's territory. "Antoine may pretend to be offended, but in reality, he will be happy for you. His kitchen is a busy one, especially later in the day."

Esther stared at him, but didn't say a word. Instead, she shoveled more of her breakfast into her mouth. In the most lady-like way possible. As she had shown him the evening before, she savored every mouthful.

And he savored watching her.

Parker had already formed a bond with his unexpected guest. He had enjoyed having her here, despite the circumstances. There was a void in his life he hadn't been able to fill. Until Esther came along.

Once again there was purpose in his life. He had something to look forward to, even if it was destined to be short-lived. When the danger was over, when those responsible were jailed, possibly hanged, Esther could, and probably would, go back to her cottage in Helena.

It made sense she would do that. She had a home there, and a job. More likely than not, she had friends and family in the area. Parker knew he needed to keep his distance, otherwise their friendship would turn into something more.

As much as he wanted to get to know her better, for his own sense of well-being, he needed to keep to a strictly friends only level.

The thought made him sigh. Esther glanced up and frowned. "Are you alright?" she asked.

"Of course," he lied. "How are you feeling today?"

She stared at him. Esther was far more astute than he'd given her credit for. No doubt the drugs were wearing off. Which of course, was what he wanted. His biggest fear was she would see right through him.

Where would he be then? He couldn't bear to have his heart broken – it was already shattered. Parker wasn't sure he would survive losing someone else he cared deeply for. Even if that someone had only recently infiltrated his life.

Chapter Eleven

Esther wasn't sure what was going on in Parker's mind, but something had him distracted. It wasn't due to her opening the door, she was certain of it.

He had assured her, more than once, that no one, other than his trusted staff, could reach the suite. The moment she knew who was at the door, she had no compulsion to keep him outside.

She had seen the looks passing between the two men. There was something much deeper between them. Apart from Antoine being Parker's brother-in-law, that was. She wondered if Antoine had married Parker's sister, or if Parker had been married to Antoine's sister.

Either way, it was none of her business.

She was only here for a week at the most, until she was fully recovered. What she would do after that, Esther really wasn't certain. Parker had indicated yesterday, he would inform the sheriff about her situation. She felt more prepared for an interrogation today, than she did yesterday. She only hoped the sheriff would come to Parker's suite.

She didn't want to be seen in town for obvious reasons. What if the brothel owner happened to track her down to Silvercrest where Parker lived?

She was convinced he would not hesitate to snatch her again. Only this time he would make certain she couldn't escape. The thing that had her baffled was why did they come after her? Esther was no longer a young woman. It was less than twelve months until her fortieth birthday. Did brothel clients want older women?

The thought churned her stomach. Bile rose in her throat, and she ran to the bathroom. Her mind was her downfall. It always had been. Or so she'd been told. Father always told Esther she should have been born male. Intelligence was wasted on women, he'd said. As it turned out, he was right.

Most men felt threatened by women who were smarter than them. Securing a job as head cook was a fluke. She was one of the few women in her cooking class. She was the only woman to graduate with honors. She felt like a cat among the pigeons. The men all had chef positions arranged before graduation day.

Esther and her female colleagues were offered only cook positions. It paid far less, and was not as prestigious as what the men were offered. It was outright discrimination, but there was nothing any of them could do.

Instead, she accepted the only available position in her beloved Helena. She was head *cook*, and paid little more than the kitchen hands, including those who washed the dishes. It was downright depressing.

"Esther? Are you alright?" Parker's voice came through the bathroom door as he knocked. "Do you need help?"

She wasn't sure what kind of help he would give her, so called back. "No. I'll be alright."

It appeared Parker stayed right where he was, since she hadn't heard movement heading back to the dining room. She glanced at her reflection, and shook her head. Her pallor was terrible. She was ghostly white. Wetting the face cloth, she wiped it over her face. The cold water helped. At least she thought it did.

Esther rinsed her mouth, ridding herself of the awful taste. She fixed her hair, then slapped her cheeks. There was now a little color in her cheeks – enough to make Parker believe she was feeling better.

She opened the door to find him still standing there, concern written all over his face. "Are you really alright?" he asked. "Should I call for the doc?"

"No!" she blurted out. "I don't need a doctor. I probably ate too much." She had no intention of telling Parker what had induced her vomiting.

Divulging her every thought would do neither of them any good. "I…need a cup of tea," she announced, right before heading back to the table.

~*~

Now she was settled in the sitting room with a fresh mug of tea, Esther felt somewhat better. Her stomach was no longer churning, and she was certain the color had come back into her face. Or perhaps the heat from the fire is what made her feel warm?

Either way, Parker wasn't studying her the way he'd done earlier. The knock at the door made her jump.

"It's Antoine," she heard him shout through the door. Parker stood, and went to the door. Moments later, Esther heard the two men talking. Well, muttering, since she couldn't make out the words. Plates rattled, as Antoine no doubt prepared the tray to take downstairs again.

Except now, the two men entered the sitting room. Parker sat opposite her as he'd done earlier, and Antoine claimed the chair beside her. "Parker tells me you wish to do some baking," he said gently. "You don't have to do that. I am pleased to prepare whatever your heart desires."

Esther studied him. Had she offended him? She didn't think so. "Did he tell you how bored I am?" she asked. "That is my only motivation. I don't like sitting around doing nothing. Besides, I'm sure you have more than enough to do."

Antoine glanced across at Parker, then returned his focus to Esther. "I won't try to talk you out of it. A woman always knows best. That's my motto."

His words made Esther laugh. "You are probably right," she said, now feeling more relaxed than earlier. "Could I give you a list of supplies? Would you mind terribly?" His face softened. Not that he was stern before, but it was as though he now understood her reasoning. Esther was certain he would be the same, given similar circumstances.

"Of course, Mademoiselle," he said, his eyes sparkling. "Who could deny a beautiful lady such as yourself."

Parker rolled his eyes. "He's like this with all the women," he said light-heartedly. "Don't be fooled by his false charm."

The two men locked eyes, then chuckled. "Do provide a list, and I will ensure it is fulfilled," Antoine told her. "In the meantime, I must away. Is there anything you need immediately?"

"Tea, and coffee? Oh, and milk," Esther said, pleased to know they could have a hot drink whenever the mood hit. "Thank you, Antoine. I truly appreciate it."

The men stood, and Esther followed suit. She felt comfortable with both men, and knew her secret was safe. Not that Antoine knew who she was or why she was here. But he seemed to understand she was in a predicament that necessitated confidentiality.

As he was readying himself to leave the suite, Antoine turned back to face her. He rubbed a hand across his chin. "Have you tried that old oven? It hasn't been used for many years, and may not even work."

Esther's heart sank. Did that mean baking was out of the question? She hoped not. She was bored beyond belief. Esther shook her head. "I've fueled it, but nothing more. I guess there is nothing to do but try it."

"Good luck with that, mon amie," Antoine said, then lifted the tray and was gone as quickly as he'd arrived.

Chapter Twelve

Parker watched as disappointment marred Esther's face. He knew how much she wanted this. Baking was to be an outlet for her boredom. He also understood it was her only motivation – she didn't plan to undermine Antoine or his staff. He was certain it hadn't even crossed her mind. "Let's go and check the oven," he said firmly. "And hope it works," he muttered under his breath. Unfortunately, not quiet enough.

"I too, hope it works," Esther countered. "Have you never used it? Not ever?"

Parker shook his head.

"How long have you lived here?" She seemed incredulous at his answer. "A number of years, isn't it?"

Parker mentally recalled the time when he moved here. When he purchased the saloon. It was years ago, but at times, it seemed like only yesterday. Especially the sorrow. It never left his mind. "I guess I was lazy," he said. "The saloon kitchen is close to my office. Antoine is an excellent chef, so it was easier to order whatever I wanted." He shrugged his shoulders, knowing he could have done better.

Esther studied him. It felt as though she could see deep into his soul. "There were unhappy times here, weren't there?" she asked gently. Then she shivered. "Don't answer that – it is none of my business."

"My sister, Charlotte, moved in with me. The guest room was originally her bedroom." Emotion still overcame him talking about it. Mostly, he simply didn't discuss it. "Antoine was already head chef here when I took over. He and Charlotte hit it off." His last words trailed off. Even after all this time, finding the words, the guilt he felt, they were still there. Instead of continuing, he headed into the kitchen to check out the stove.

Parker felt Esther's gaze burn into his back. His entire body was rigid, no matter how much he tried to relax. When they arrived in the kitchen, the room was filled with smoke. How they hadn't noticed, Parker wasn't sure. Perhaps his emotions were the culprit. They blocked out everything else. This wasn't the first time. "I think we have our answer," he said.

"I'm sorry," Esther said. "I shouldn't have lit the stove without knowing if it was functional. I had no reason to think it wasn't."

Parker crossed the floor and opened a window. He threw water on the burning fire, extinguishing it. The smoke began to dissipate. "It's probably the flue," he said. "I can have it cleaned. Or maybe not," he added. "Given the circumstances."

Pounding on the door startled him, and he hurried out to see who is was.

"It's Antoine. You have a fire!" he said urgently.

Parker quickly opened the door. "We have smoke," he told the chef. "Looks like you were right about that old oven. It can probably be repaired, but I don't want strangers here at the moment."

Antoine studied him. "I think it's time you told me what is going on," he said as he crossed his arms and stared at Parker. "Now would be a good time," he said firmly.

~*~

As the three sat in the sitting room, Antoine listened carefully. He nodded now and then but said nothing until Parker finished relaying Esther's story at her request.

Antoine's eyes opened in astonishment. "Déjà vu, mon ami." Antoine said gently once Parker finished speaking. He studied Esther. "And you, my dear. How are you?"

Esther writhed in her chair. It was easy to see she didn't like being the subject of the discussion. Instead of answering Antoine's direct question, she asked one of her own. "What do you mean it's déjà vu?"

Very little got past Esther. He had thought it before, but now Parker was convinced she was far more astute than she was given credit for. He locked eyes with Antoine. His brother-in-law moved his head ever so slightly, but Parker recognized it as permission to tell Charlotte's story.

"Your situation," Parker said quietly, "almost mirrors what happened to Charlotte. Except she disappeared and we had no idea what happened."

Antoine added, "Until it was too late." He ran a hand through his hair before speaking again. "Charlotte and I were to marry less than a week later," he said, his voice full of emotion. "They kidnapped her and we never saw her again." He wiped a tear from his eyes, not even trying to hide his distress.

"Until her body was found," Parker added. "The sheriff wasn't convinced she'd been taken by Brutus Ahearn, the brothel owner in Johnsonville. He was known for…" He shifted in his seat. "Well, you know the rest."

"The sheriff refused to believe what was right before his eyes," Antoine snarled. "The man is a criminal."

The atmosphere in the room was suddenly one of absolute anguish. Parker glanced at Esther. She hadn't said anything since they'd begun to relay the story of Charlotte's demise. Tears streamed down her face. Parker knew her tears were not for herself, but for Charlotte, and the two men in the room with her.

"You knew what happened to me, didn't you?" she demanded of Parker. "It's the reason you helped me." She swiped a hand across her face, but her tears continued to fall.

"I would have helped you regardless. No one has the right to take away another person's choice. To dictate the way they live. Unfortunately, it appears he is still operating under the same system."

"He has to be stopped," Esther said firmly, then stood. "I need to speak with the sheriff. I'm ready now."

Parker and Antoine exchanged looks. "He must be stopped," Antoine said gently. "But I'm not convinced our sheriff is the one to do it."

"In other words," Esther said firmly, "he has the law in his pocket. That needs to change, and I'm ready to see it happens."

Parker opened his mouth to speak, then snapped it closed. Antoine did the same. They were both speechless. What did this petite woman think she could do that no one else had been able to achieve?

Chapter Thirteen

For a fleeting moment, Esther believed the two men thought her a foolish woman. Someone who had no clout.

They were wrong.

She might not be in law enforcement, but when Brutus Ahearn had her kidnapped for his brothel, he picked the wrong woman. When she was done with him, the brothel owner would wish he'd never been born.

Esther took a deep and fortifying breath. Then she stood.

She paced the room, all the time two pairs of eyes burned a hole in her back.

"Esther." She could hear the anguish in Parker's voice. He was concerned about her. "Esther," he said, this time far more tenderly. "I'm worried about you."

She turned to face him. "Don't concern yourself about my welfare. It's Brutus Ahearn you should worry about."

Both Parker and Antoine scowled. "What do you plan to do, mon amie?" Antoine asked, his voice soft. "The law can handle this."

"No, they can't," she snapped, not meaning to. "It is clear they have been unable to eliminate this excuse for a man." The words came out as a growl. It wasn't what she intended. Esther did some more deep breathing. "My head is clear now. The drugs appear to be out of my system."

When neither man spoke, Esther continued. "I know someone who would be more than willing to rid the world of this abhorrent and evil man." She knew what they were both thinking. That Esther was a mere woman. A small one at that. Admittedly, she appeared to be nothing more than a frightened woman. To outsiders, she likely seemed to be all talk and no action, but now her mind was clearer. Now Esther knew exactly what she needed to do.

First though, the sheriff needed a statement, even if Parker and Antoine believed he couldn't be trusted. Only then could she put her plan into action.

Esther wasn't ready to show herself on the streets of Silvercrest. Not yet anyway.

Sheriff Peter Dodd was summoned to Parker's suite, and it wasn't long before he arrived. "What's this about, Parker?" the sheriff demanded. Clearly annoyed at being called away from his office.

"Take a seat, Sheriff," Esther told him as she motioned to the chair nearest the blazing fire. "I need to report a kidnapping."

"Humph!" the sheriff said. "And who's kidnapping might that be?" The man scowled, and it was apparent he believed his time was being wasted.

"Mine," Esther said firmly. "I was kidnapped and drugged by the brothel owner, Brutus Ahearn. I'm sure you know of him. His brothel is in Johnsonville." She watched the sheriff carefully for his reaction. If her new friends were right, he would try to brush her off as an overwrought woman.

As expected, the sheriff was indifferent to her claim. His head snapped up, and his eyes immediately met Parker's. "I've never heard of anyone escaping his clutches," he said, with disbelief in his voice. "I can take your statement, but I can't do much. It's simply a waste of my time. He is not from around here, and hasn't broken any laws in Silvercrest."

"You *will* take my statement," Esther said firmly, "and then you will do exactly what I say. If it's the last thing I do, I will bring that beast and his brothel down. I will ensure the women who are held captive there are all released and reunited with their families."

"And exactly how do you intend to do that?" Sheriff Dodd asked, amusement in his voice.

Esther thought she couldn't be more riled up than she already was. She was wrong. "Do you think because I am a woman, I can't make things happen? Then you would be completely wrong."

She let her words sink in before continuing. "Sheriff Dodd," Esther said firmly. "You have no doubt heard of Robert Carnal."

Now the sheriff appeared confused. "The Chief of the US Marshals? Of course. What does he have to do with this situation?"

"Robert Carnal, Robbie, is my step-brother. My very protective step-brother who is more like a full sibling than a step. We grew up together."

The sheriff's face lost all color. The man stuttered at the sheer shock of her statement. "He…he's your brother?" He turned to face Parker. "Is this true?" he demanded, although no longer in complete control of his reactions.

Esther couldn't have hoped for more. The sheriff was now terrified – he'd got away with his illegal activities for far too long. She planned to have him stopped. Robbie could certainly do that.

Parker shrugged. "I had no idea," he said, then glanced at Esther, his eyes silently questioning her. "If Esther said it, then it's true," Parker said, irritation clear in his tone. "What do you suggest we do now, Esther?" he asked, ignoring the sheriff.

Esther though for mere seconds. "I will send a telegraph to Robbie. It will take some days for him to get here, but he will come, I have no doubt."

Sheriff Dodd looked none too happy about her suggestion. He opened his mouth to protest, then snapped it shut. He already looked like a fool, and apparently decided not to risk any further embarrassment. "Shall we move to the dining room for you to take down my statement?" Esther tried to keep the annoyance out of her voice, but failed miserably. "When you leave, I'll work on my message to Robbie." Her eyes never left the sheriff's face. He nodded briefly, then stood. Parker led him to the dining room, and Esther relayed what happened, and provided every detail she could remember.

The sheriff hurriedly scribbled down her words, trying to keep up.

"Not a word about this to anyone," Esther told the sheriff. "I'm sure Robbie will inform you of what is required of the sheriff's office here in Silvercrest. Until then, not a word. Not even to your deputy."

"But I…" He stopped speaking the moment Esther scowled. "Of course," he said, snatching up his notebook. "I will wait to hear from…your brother," he said. The last words on a snarl. It was all Esther could do not to laugh. She glanced across at Parker, who had covered his mouth with his hand. It was blatantly clear he was amused, but had no intention of showing it.

Almost the moment the door closed behind the sheriff, Esther breathed a sigh of relief. She was convinced Antoine was right – the man was associated with the brothel owner. More likely than not, he was instrumental in finding women for Brutus Ahearn.

"You don't think it would have been better to keep the information about your brother to yourself? Assuming what you said was true, and not bluff?" Parker seemed quite concerned.

"Oh it's true," Esther told him. "All except the time frame it would take for Robbie to get here. I can almost guarantee he will be here before Dodd can get a message to Ahearn."

Parker studied her. "You're trying to draw them all out, aren't you? Beating Dodd at his own game."

"And Ahearn," she said firmly. "He is the main catch, but it would be nice to get the small fry, too. Those women need rescuing."

Chapter Fourteen

At first he was amazed at Esther's revelations. Her demands to the sheriff more than surprised him, they shocked him. Finding out her brother was Chief of the US Marshals? That stunned him. Sheriff Dodd was equally amazed. Or perhaps it was more concern?

Parker studied Esther. Was this really the placid and frightened woman who escaped the clutches of a notorious brothel owner? He hadn't imagined she'd leaped onto the stagecoach Parker happened to be in; she really did that. He was a witness to her close escape from one of the most evil men who ever walked this earth.

"You're full of surprises," he said.

Esther gazed at him. He wondered what she was thinking. "The man's an idiot," she said gruffly. "Lazy at the least." She headed into the sitting room and took the seat by the fire. "He gave me the chills. I know Antoine does, but do you also think he's involved with the brothel in some way?"

It wasn't a scenario Parker had considered. At the time of Charlotte's passing, he'd brushed Antoine's accusations aside. Now, he couldn't help but frown. "Honestly? I don't know," he said. "He's always been a strange one. Charlotte's murder was never investigated the way Antoine and I believed it should be."

"In what way?" Esther asked gently.

"He ruled it an accident. Except it was no accident. Antoine and I spent months trying to locate Charlotte. We checked everywhere. Except the one place she turned out to be in."

Pain hit him right in the chest. His heart was still shattered at what happened.

"None of this is your fault, or Antoine's. You know that, right?" She gazed at him. Her eyes never leaving his face.

"I know, but it doesn't stop the pain, or the guilt."

Esther went to Parker and put her arms around him. He and Antoine comforted each other when they deemed it necessary. They might not be blood, and were not truly family, but they might as well be. They'd been through so much together.

She held him tight, her arms around his back. Reluctantly at first, Parker's arms circled her small body. That this petite woman could bring so much comfort, and be so commanding, was a revelation he hadn't expected.

"We shouldn't be doing this," Parker whispered. Esther stepped back, and he regretted his words. He'd enjoyed holding her. He knew he shouldn't, but couldn't help it.

Besides, it meant nothing. They were comforting each other. Nothing more, and nothing less.

"There are times," Esther said firmly, "when we all need the comfort of a friend. I consider you a friend, and I can see you need my support right now." Instead of moving away, Esther moved into him again, and wrapped him in her arms. Parker didn't say a word, but let his heart rule. His arms snaked up and around her, and Esther's head rested against his shoulder.

It was very clear, perhaps to them both, each needed the comfort of the other at this moment. Parker vowed to ensure it didn't happen again, but for now, he was right where he wanted to be.

"It's been an eventful day," Esther announced when she finally stepped out of his arms.

Parker knew he shouldn't, but he felt…empty, when she moved away. He seemed to have some sort of affinity with the woman he'd befriended to ensure her safety. Bringing Sheriff Dodd here seemed the right thing to do. Now he wasn't so sure.

"If I can have something to write on, I'll get a message to my brother. I know Robbie will want to get this sorted."

Parker was certain she was right. It was personal for him, with both Charlotte and Esther, and he could only imagine Esther's brother's reaction. Even a step-brother would not be thrilled at the news. In his situation, Robert Carnal had the means to ensure it never happened to another woman without her consent.

He couldn't imagine many women wanting to become soiled doves, but knew it to be true. There were those who were desperate for money to support themselves, and even their families. But kidnapping and forcing women into that life was not only illegal, but immoral.

If Parker were able to put a stop to it, he would do his utmost. Anything he was able to contribute to the downfall of corrupt brothel owners everywhere, would be welcomed with open arms.

Dealing with corrupt sheriffs – that was a different thing altogether. He was in two minds about Sheriff Peter Dodd. He had not conducted a thorough investigation into Charlotte's murder. Instead he maintained it was an accident. How he came to that conclusion, Parker had no idea. The sheriff refused to share his findings.

Parker's biggest fear now, was if the lawman destroyed any and all paperwork related to Charlotte's disappearance and death. In the meantime, he had to continue as normal. Assume the sheriff's innocence, despite his reservations about the man.

He would update Antoine when next he saw him, knowing he would have enjoyed the show Esther put on. She had gone from a wallflower to a powerhouse in a matter of moments. It was clear to him, Esther was far more than she let on.

~*~

After several drafts of her telegraph message, Esther finally handed him the message.

It read, *Your Star misses you. Let's have lunch at the Silvercrest Saloon. Bring some friends.*

Parker read it, and read it again. "He'll understand this?" he asked. The message made no sense whatsoever to Parker.

Esther studied him momentarily. "Star is Robbie's pet name for me. I've told him where to come, and he needs reinforcements. I promise he'll understand."

Parker still wasn't convinced but had to trust Esther's opinion. "I can take this to the telegraph office, but it will be obvious to the sheriff if he's watching. Besides, I don't want to leave you alone."

Soon afterward, there was a knock at the door. "It's Antoine," he called through the door.

The aroma of the various pastries and beverages hit his senses the moment the door opened. Placing the tray on the table, he lingered. No doubt wanting an update.

Parker had always intended to keep Antoine informed. He wasn't certain his brother-in-law would be impressed with the turn of events.

Chapter Fifteen

It wasn't until Antoine removed everything from the tray Esther noticed the additional mug. He had obviously planned to stay and find out the latest.

"You missed a wonderful show," Parker said, grinning at Esther.

She studied him. "It wasn't a show – I was putting that fool in his place. Besides, Robbie can bring Brutus Ahearn down, I am certain of it. If he can do the same for the sheriff, so be it."

She took a sip of tea, trying to slow her heart rate again. She had calmed herself earlier, while she wrote the message for Robbie. But discussing the sheriff and his ridiculous behavior, had her churned up once again.

Antoine pushed the plate of pastries toward her. "Ladies first," he said. It made Esther wonder if her annoyance was showing. "I made these especially, so you must eat them. Light on the tummy too," he added, as though he believed he was helping with her health.

"You make the best pastries," Parker said, then reached for a pastry once Esther had made her choice.

Moments later, after being filled in on the discussion, Antoine frowned. "Who is Robbie?" he asked, as though it had just dawned on him.

"He's my step-brother," Esther told him. "He's also the Chief of the US Marshals."

Antoine's eyes opened in astonishment. "And he will help?" His words sounded as though he wasn't entirely convinced.

"I have no doubt about it," Esther told him. "I am sending a cryptic telegraph. I hope it gets him here quickly."

Antoine reached for the telegraph. "I can send this straight away. On second thought, I will send one of my waiters, that way it won't be obvious."

"You don't trust the sheriff," Esther said firmly. "I don't either."

"Oui. I do not trust that man. He was useless when our Charlotte died."

"Robbie will get to the truth, I'm certain."

Antoine chuckled. "He loves his sister, as he should." He drank down the last of his coffee. "I will go. The sooner your message is sent, the better." He glanced at the words again, ensuring all necessary information was provided.

Parker reached into his pocket, pulling out a note. "Give him this. Tell him to buy the telegraph operator's silence."

Antoine stared at him. "You believe it's necessary? Of course you do," he said, then stood. "It will be done," he said firmly, then left them alone.

Esther's head was in a spin. In the last hour, she had learned the only two people she trusted did not believe their local sheriff was honest.

Almost the second Parker closed the door behind the chef, Esther felt somewhat relieved. Although she wouldn't fool herself. It was a difficult situation getting that telegraph message sent. If the sheriff got wind it was her sending the message, Esther was convinced he would intercept it.

Had she put one of the saloon's waiters in danger? Or anyone else? She felt a headache coming on. If it was only her being affected, it wouldn't matter. Except that was far from the case. Anyone she had come into contact with here in town was potentially in danger. Even the doctor.

More likely than not, if he was in the pocket of the brothel owner, Sheriff Dodd had already informed him Esther was here. It wasn't ideal, but she had little choice. To get Robbie here, she had no choice but to get a message to him. He could feasibly arrive in town by late tomorrow. Hopefully with several other marshals.

Esther sighed. If he traveled all night he would get here more quickly. Either way, he wouldn't arrive until the next day. Despite the time it would take, she felt as though some of the weight had been lifted from her shoulders. Robbie would come, she knew he would. The sooner the better as far as she was concerned.

~*~

The rest of the day had passed slowly. Antoine reported the message had been sent, and there was no record whatsoever of the sender. It had to be a positive. Now to wait.

She barely slept, and merely tossed and turned throughout the night. Not only did she not sleep, but she heard Parker pacing the sitting room floor. In the end, she couldn't stand trying to sleep when she knew it simply wouldn't happen.

Parker was tending to the sitting room fire when she joined him. She was in her nightgown and robe, and did feel rather self-conscious about it. Parker on the other hand, wore only his trousers. The shock of seeing him like that was so great, Esther gasped.

Even back when they were children, Esther had never seen her brother in a state of undress. She was far too young when her own father died to remember anything back then. Mother was inconsolable until Robbie's father came along and saved them from starvation and destitution. At least that's what Robbie told her. Esther could only believe it was true.

Parker turned at the intrusion of what he apparently believed would be him alone. "Forgive my state of undress," he said quickly, then abandoned the fire to cover himself up. When he returned, Parker wore a shirt, which now covered his perfectly sculptured body.

Esther couldn't deny she was at first shocked, but had also enjoyed seeing his beautiful body. Were all men built like this? She had led such a sheltered life. Robbie had ensured she was protected from the evil of the world. Except it hadn't saved her from the wicked brothel owner.

Had she understood the ways of the world, perhaps she would have been more cautious. She began to condemn her own actions, but recalled the words Parker had said. He questioned why the diner owner did not escort her home in the darkness.

Esther now realized it was a perfectly good question. Except she likely wouldn't return to Helena after what had happened. She knew she was within her rights to feel this way. So far she felt safe here in Silvercrest. Whether that would be the case down the track remained to be seen.

She certainly had no intention of making any decisions until Robbie arrived.

"I wish I could make tea for us both," she said when Parker returned, trying to fill the void in the quiet room. "Except it's probably too dangerous."

"We can go down to the kitchen," he said. "The kitchen is also in the locked area. No one can enter unless they have the keys. At least when we are closed," he added.

"Oh, I didn't know," Esther said, still interested in making tea.

"Tea would be nice but not essential. I'll take you down, in just a few minutes. Let me finish getting this fire going first."

Esther stared at him. "You don't want tea?"

"I don't want you to feel you have to make tea," he said.

Esther sat down in one of the chairs, instead of standing and feeling as though she didn't belong.

Parker turned to face her. "I am ready now," he said and stepped toward her. Esther stood, and the two collided. She toppled sideways, and put out her arms to stop herself falling. Parker grabbed her at the same time.

They were face to face, and somehow became entwined. She glanced up into his face, and a strange feeling came over her. She gazed into his brown eyes. They reminded her of a puppy she had as a child. Except in those eyes she saw sadness. A look of hopelessness.

All because of her. She was ready to flee, make him happy again. The feeling she had was so strong to leave him alone with his grief. Except she didn't want to leave his arms. Not ever.

Instead, she did the only other sensible thing she could do. Esther went up on her toes, and kissed Parker. He didn't resist. Instead, he kissed her back.

What Robbie would say, she really wasn't sure.

Chapter Sixteen

Parker was stunned, but only momentarily.

Esther had done what he'd only dreamed about. She kissed him. He had not even thought about love for a very long time. Charlotte's death had shattered his entire being. His life. If not for Antoine, he had no idea where he would be now. Dead most likely.

Losing Charlotte had destroyed them both. They supported each other through the difficult times of not knowing where she was, and the weeks and months after they did. If not for Charlotte slipping a note in her corset, they would have had no clue where she'd been.

When Parker and Antoine had found her body, they'd carried her to Doc Billings office. He'd pronounced her dead, and the sheriff was called. At no point did Sheriff Dodd accept her death as more than an accident.

Even when the doc found the note, the sheriff still refused to accept it as more than a tragic accident. Why then, did he not call the sheriff out then? If he had, perhaps Esther, and who knew how many other women, would not have been kidnapped in the same set of circumstances.

Parker shook himself mentally. He had to focus on the present. And that present was more than a little pleasant. Except…was he taking advantage of Esther's delicate state of mind? No matter she made the first move, it made him wonder if she had the capacity to make such a decision. A shiver went down his spine when her hand cupped his cheek.

"Is something wrong?" she asked him quietly.

He glanced down into her beautiful face. "Wrong? Nothing is wrong," he said. "It's just…"

She studied him before speaking again. "If you're worried about Robbie, don't. I'm a big girl, I can make my own decisions. If you're worried about taking advantage of me, again, don't. As I've already said, I am more than capable of deciding what I should and shouldn't do. Neither you, or Robbie have a say in that."

If this had not happened today, it would be a different story. Previously, her mind had been blocked by the drugs she was force-fed. Her interaction with Sheriff Dodd proved that was no longer the case. She was astute, and as such, could hold her own.

It was clear to Parker, the sheriff had not known what hit him. He was blindsided by the woman the sheriff had assumed to be a fool. Instead, he quickly discovered Esther was far from it. Not to mention she had a brother who would assure justice was done. Not only for Esther, but for Charlotte and every other woman ever taken by the brothel owner and his men.

This was, provided the sheriff did not alert Brutus Ahearn. If it happened, they would know for certain the sheriff of Silvercrest was dirty and on the payroll of the brothel owner. It meant they could trust no one outside of their little circle of Antoine, Esther, and himself.

"Parker? What is going on in your head?" Esther's voice cut through his thoughts. Instead of waiting for an answer, she kissed him again. This time the kiss was not fast, and it was far from chaste. It was done with intent.

Her arms snaked up around him, and Parker couldn't help but do the same. Esther meant far more to him than he'd ever intended. He wasn't sure when the transition from rescuer happened, but she was now much more than a damsel in distress who was hiding out in his suite.

Her lips on his were pure bliss. Parker couldn't help but respond in kind. His arms circled her body, and he pulled her closer. In those moments, Parker knew he was right where he needed to be.

He also knew this was a turning point in their relationship. At least it's how he saw it. Whether it was a fleeting attraction for Esther, he did not know. It seemed less than ideal, especially since once the brothel owner was in jail, Esther was sure to go back to her life in Helena. She wouldn't want to stay here in Silvercrest.

Why would she? There was nothing here for her. Being here with Parker was fine while it lasted, and he was certainly enjoying it, but would it continue? Esther seemed to be concerned her brother may not be impressed about their relationship. With her staying here with him, an unmarried man.

He would feel the same. Parker had always been protective of Charlotte, and as it turned out, he was right to be concerned about his sister's welfare. Had she moved in with a man, a total stranger as Esther had done, through no fault of her own, he would have not been pleased.

"We really shouldn't," he whispered, and Esther pulled back. She glanced up into his face.

"If you're worried about Robbie, don't be. If there is something else that is bothering you, tell me now." She gazed into his face, and seemed to be waiting for an answer. Instead he shrugged his shoulders.

"If I were your brother," he said, gazing down into her face, "I would not be happy about us living together." What he didn't say was the part about Robbie having the means to bring him down. If he was anything like Esther, Parker had nothing to worry about, but Robbie was the Chief of the US Marshals. It meant he was ruthless, and took no nonsense from anyone. Especially not unknown men who had ulterior motives toward his sister. Not that Parker was behaving like that.

Either way, Parker was certain words would pass between the men. Not necessarily good ones.

He could see the frustration on Esther's face. She opened her mouth to speak, at the same time, there was a knock on the door.

"It's Antoine," he called out.

Esther rolled her eyes. "Does he never go home?" she asked, then smiled.

At least Parker knew she was joking. But she was right – Antoine spent far too long at work. Perhaps for the same reason Parker did. To retain his sanity.

Opening the door introduced delicious aromas, as it always did. Antoine always ensured Parker's meals were the best available, just as he did for the saloon. Parker ran a high level restaurant. He had always planned to change the name of his establishment to anything other than saloon. It was a task he'd never got around to doing.

The business was losing money when he took it over, and the only decent part of it was the owner's suite. The saloon was all but destroyed from all the drunks and bar fights. He had put a stop to those activities, and removed alcohol from the beverages available. Meals provided by Antoine were the drawcard, and it had pulled in a far higher standard of clientele.

He recalled those early days. It was constant hard work restoring the building to its former glory, not to mention a heap of money. But retore it he did, along with completely removing the bar. Drunks were refused entry.

All that was left to do now was rename the saloon and remove the last evidence of its sordid past. Perhaps Esther would help him come up with a suitable name.

Then again, her brother would likely take her home with him until the danger was over. The mere thought of it shattered his heart into a million pieces.

Chapter Seventeen

Esther couldn't stay mad with Antoine. Not that she ever was, not really.

"Good evening," Antoine said, as he placed their meals on the dining table. "Tonight you have Chicken Chasseur. Very light on the stomach, while also filling the belly and providing much needed nourishment."

They never did get around to making refreshments in the kitchen, but Esther didn't mind. She had enjoyed kissing Parker, even if he had been reluctant at first. Except he was still holding back, and she was certain it was because of Robbie. What Parker didn't seem to understand was she could wrap Robbie around her little finger. He might come across as the protective big brother, which he totally was, but she could always talk him around.

Besides, she was a grown woman who made her own decisions. Robbie knew it, but still tried to push her around. For her own good, he always said, but it made no difference to Esther. All she had to do was smile, and hug her brother, and he would back off. The very thought of it made her smile.

"What is making you smile, Mademoiselle Esther?" Antoine asked, his curiosity peaked.

His question made her chuckle. "I was thinking about my brother. Robbie can come across as a bit of a tyrant when it comes to me, but he's a pushover. You'll see." She smiled again, then sat down. "If I know my brother, he'll be here sooner than later. He'll likely drive through the night." She sighed then. He could be rather pig-headed at times. Especially when he believed his little sister to be in danger.

Antoine served their food from a terrine. Mashed potatoes followed. Esther leaned forward and breathed in the exquisite aroma. "Enjoy," he said, then began to walk away.

"You're not joining us?" Esther asked. "I've not seen you eat since I arrived here. Where and when do you have your meals?" She was genuinely curious. Not once had she seen Antoine partake of the wonderful food he served.

At her question, Antoine seemed to squirm. Parker frowned. "It's a good question," Parker said. "When do you eat, and where?" he asked.

"What do you mean? I eat when I feel hungry." As if on cue, his stomach growled, and Antoine rolled his eyes, then turned away.

"Please," Esther pleaded, "fetch a plate and cutlery and join us." She watched as a frown marred his face. "I refuse to eat if you don't join us," she said firmly, crossing her arms in front of herself. She glared at Parker when he chuckled.

"Best do what she says," Parker told Antoine. "I'm beginning to see why Robbie is so forceful with his little sister," he said, a grin on his face.

Antoine shrugged his shoulders, and went downstairs. He was back in record time.

~*~

"The meal was wonderful, Antoine," Esther said. "And all the better for the wonderful company. Robbie will be grateful to you both for looking after me."

Parker frowned. "Are you certain?" he asked. "If I were in his shoes, I'd be furious. A strange man taking his sister in with no chaperone."

Esther held her hand up. "Stop," she said firmly. "My life, my choice. Robbie has never had a say in what I do, not even when we were younger."

"Exactly how much older than you is he?" Parker asked, with trepidation in his voice.

Esther couldn't stop herself from laughing. "One hundred and twenty-five days." She had always seen it as a huge joke. Robbie her big brother, was only a few months older than her. "Many people believed we were twins. Of course we're not, but it didn't stop the tongues wagging."

The two men stared at her. "Our parents were all close friends. Robbie's mother had died a few years earlier, then my father died. According to Robbie's father, it made sense for them to marry. Mother agreed, and soon afterwards, they did. We moved into the Carnal home, and the rest is history.

"How old were you when they married?" Parker wanted to know.

Esther wasn't sure it was relevant, but perhaps Parker believed it was. "We were twelve," she said quietly. "It was a difficult time for both of us, and we came to rely on each other. Robbie played the big brother very well, and decided he would never give up the role."

"Boyfriends?" Parker said, not needing to elaborate.

She sighed. "Not many. Each potential boyfriend was closely vetted by Robbie. Most walked away."

"I can totally relate to that," Parker said quietly. Antoine nodded. Both men had been through so much. Losing Charlotte had clearly changed both their lives.

Antoine stood then, and began to pack up the dishes. Esther covered his hand with her own. "You and

Parker take your coffee to the sitting room. I've got this."

"Oh no, mon amie. This is my job."

"Not tonight. Now do as you are told," Esther said firmly, then took over the task. Shrugging his shoulders, Antoine understood it was a lost cause and he wouldn't win this battle.

With the room to herself, Esther began to clear the table. After spending many years doing the same job as Antoine, she understood what it felt like to be under appreciated. To always be looking after other people, and not taking the same care with your own well-being.

Antoine had taken special care of her health by ensuring the meals he served did not upset her stomach. Esther appreciated it far more than he would ever know. Clearing the table was the least she could do. He was a sweet man, and this was one of the few ways she knew to repay him.

Finally finished, she poured herself a cup of tea, then headed into the sitting room to spend time with her two new friends.

She would enjoy the peace and quiet with them while she could. Esther knew once her brother arrived, all hell would break loose. Neither man would know what hit them.

Chapter Eighteen

It had taken Parker forever to fall asleep. He was deeply worried about Robbie's response to the current situation Esther found herself in. Not that he had anything to hide, because he didn't.

The fact they'd fallen for each other was the area of concern. Would Robbie believe they genuinely loved each other? Or would he automatically believe Parker had used the situation to entice and trick his sister?

Putting himself in Robbie's shoes, Parker would definitely think the worse. He would not believe a word he said, and would quickly jump to conclusions. Esther told him not to worry about Robbie, but how could he not? It seemed, without having met the man, Robbie was more than a little protective of his little sister. Even if she was not a child anymore, and hadn't been for at least two decades.

Still, it had not stopped him worrying about Charlotte. And rightly so. He only hoped Robbie didn't break down any doors trying to get to him.

Of course, he wouldn't be alone. If he took notice of Esther's telegraph, that is.

Now he was certain – there would be a barrage of marshals with her brother. They would ensure Esther's safety, and he may never see her again. His heart sank. Was it true, or was he worrying over nothing?

It was yet to be seen.

Parker was wide awake now, and couldn't get back to sleep. Perhaps a warm cup of tea would help. He could go down to the kitchen and make one. The sun was rising, his favorite part of the day. More likely than not, Antoine would be downstairs already, working on the breakfast rush.

He really needed to find someone to help his brother-in-law and best friend. The man worked far too much, and had no private life. Parker knew it was the way Antoine preferred it, but it couldn't continue. It wasn't good to do little more than work. He knew this first-hand.

One day Antoine might even meet someone he wanted to marry. Parker would be happy for him. He deserved happiness more than anyone else Parker knew.

Finally, he gave in and climbed out of bed.

After dressing, Parker moved around the suite as quietly as he could. Esther needed her sleep, today especially. With the excitement of her brother coming to town, she would likely be exhausted by day's end. Parker on the other hand was petrified of the reaction he would receive from Robbie. Despite his best intentions, he could see how the marshal chief could misinterpret his intentions.

It wasn't every day a man got to help a lady in desperate need of rescuing, and he would not apologize for that. He also wouldn't make an apology for hiding her away in his private suite. It was the least he could do.

And besides, it was in Esther's best interest to keep her away from prying eyes. Surely Robbie would understand that? Parker could only hope, and beg forgiveness if he didn't.

He stood staring out the window. It truly was beautiful at this hour of the day. Watching the sun rise was a favorite part of the day for him, but he often did so from his office downstairs. Apart from Antoine clattering about in the large kitchen, no one else was around. There was always paperwork to do, and he was always more productive without all the interruptions he had later in the day.

Transforming the rundown saloon into a respectable restaurant had not been easy. Keeping the drunks away had been a costly exercise. Employing security was the only thing that worked – those drunks didn't give in easily. Buying the rundown building for almost nothing meant he had the capitol to turn it into his dream restaurant. Inheriting Antoine was the first step toward that goal.

Parker spun around at movement behind him. Until recently, he didn't carry a firearm. He hadn't felt the need for some time. Not since he'd moved to Silvercrest. When his sister was abducted, all that changed. Anger had overtaken him when her body was found, but he came to realize anger and guns don't mix. He had locked his gun in the small safe hidden in the bedroom.

Until now. With the threat against Esther, and the suspicion about Sheriff Dodd, he had removed it from the safe. His Colt had been in close proximity ever since. Hidden under his jacket during the day, and under his pillow at night, he wondered what Esther would think if she knew.

"Good morning," she said sleepily, then came to stand beside him. Together they stared at the beauty of the new day.

Parker glanced down at her. "Can't sleep?" he asked, and put his arm around her shoulder, pulling her closer. It was an automatic action, he hadn't thought about it until now. Esther was smiling. Did that mean she approved? He leaned in and kissed her forehead. She still didn't complain.

Parker knew he shouldn't be so forward, except it was Esther who had made the first move. Last night, he was uncertain about her motivation. He now understood she felt the same way he did.

Smitten.

With the two being forced into close contact with each other, it was inevitable they would feel this way. Except Parker knew there was far more to it. He'd never believed in fate. How could two people meant to be together find each other through fate? It seemed implausible. And yet, here they were.

Forced together by the evil actions of one man. A man Parker intended to see caught and hopefully hanged.

"Tossed and turned all night," Esther said, her voice still quiet. "And you?" She reached up and brushed the sleep from her eyes. As he gazed into her face, Parker knew he could happily watch her do this every day for the rest of his life.

Visions of her sleeping peacefully beside him drifted into his mind. When he'd watched over her that first night, it was all nightmares and terror. He never wanted her to go through a night like that again. Parker would protect her. He would hold her in his arms all night long and reassure Esther that everything would be alright.

First though, he had to get past her gatekeeper – her big brother, Robbie. The mere thought had him trembling.

Chapter Nineteen

"Tea?" Parker asked, and Esther was confused. "I thought we could go downstairs to the kitchen and make ourselves tea. Or coffee," he added with a grin. Esther had not once seen Parker drink tea since she'd arrived.

"It's safe?" she asked. It would be the first time she stepped outside the safety of Parker's suite since she'd arrived some days earlier. Not that she was complaining, because she wasn't. Esther had longed to see the kitchen Antoine worked his magic in.

Back at the diner in Helena, she worked in a pokey room that was a poor excuse for a kitchen. There was barely room for her to move around, let alone the young woman who was employed as her assistant. Esther wondered how Shelly was getting on without her.

Parker reached for her hand and squeezed it. "It's safe. The restaurant is locked up tight, and the kitchen will be empty. Apart from Antoine, that is. More likely than not, he'll be there."

Esther knew the man worked long hours, but this was ridiculous. She couldn't blame Parker. She'd seen with her own eyes, Parker begging him to go home. She knew what he was doing - Antoine was using work as a way of keeping busy. Being occupied all the time meant there was no time to think. To dwell on the bad things that happened to Charlotte.

Frankly, she didn't blame him.

Esther looked down at herself. She had dressed and was presentable in that way. She ran a hand through her hair. "Give me a moment?" Without waiting for an answer, she scurried off to the bathroom to fashion her hair into something more presentable. Staring at her reflection she gasped. She was a mess.

Esther splashed cold water on her face, and dried it using one of the luxurious towels. She brushed her hair, and pulled it into a small bun at the back of her head. Now she was ready for the day. And definitely ready for a mug of hot tea.

They slipped quietly down the stairs. Every step she took, Parker was there with her. When they reached the last step, he leaned forward and unlocked the door. It either had to be unlocked from this side, or with a key on the other side. Now she'd seen how it worked, she did feel far more secure.

He carefully locked the door behind them, and led her to the kitchen. Surprisingly, there was a passage way that went to the kitchen. "This was already here when I bought the place. It means not having to walk through the restaurant area to get to the kitchen, and also my office," he explained. "Antoine does not have to deal with the public unless he wants to."

"And does he?" she asked, curiously. Then shook her head. "Don't answer. It's not my business."

Parker grinned. "He does. When a compliment comes from a customer, he wants to meet them. He is rather vain at times." He chuckled then, and Esther knew he'd not said it in a derogatory way. Parker was merely stating fact.

At the end of the passageway, they came to another door. It was closed but not locked. Opening the door carefully, the kitchen opened out in front of them. Esther gasped.

This would have to be the largest kitchen she'd ever had the pleasure to see. It was even larger than the kitchen at the culinary school where she'd studied. She glanced about until she spotted Antoine. He was busy preparing for the breakfast rush. Suddenly his head shot up. "Ah, good morning," he said with a grin. "I thought you would still be sleeping."

"I need coffee," Parker said.

Esther smiled. She was certain he didn't drink tea. "I need tea," she said. "But I will prepare both. You carry on," she added. "Just point me in the right direction." What she really wanted to say was she adored this kitchen, and wished she could cook in it. She knew whatever she made here would be better than anything she'd ever baked before.

"You like my kitchen, no?" Antoine asked, his face now more animated than she'd ever seen.

She glanced up at Parker who was also grinning. "It's his pride and joy," Parker said. "You couldn't drag him away from it if you tried."

Warmth filled her. If this kitchen was hers, Esther would be full of happiness too. "I can see why," she said, then glanced around trying to locate the kettle. "Ah, there it is," she said and headed toward the stove.

"It is not yet boiling," Antoine said, as he finished preparing croissants for the breakfast crowd. "Why don't you show Esther the restaurant while you wait?" Antoine suggested.

"I'd love to see it," she almost squealed. It was closed now, and no risk to her safety. Her heart fluttered in anticipation. She would take advantage of this quiet time before the restaurant opened, and before her brother arrived.

The moment Robbie, along with his marshals hit Silvercrest, Esther knew it would be bedlam. She loved her brother tremendously, but when he worried about her, he had been known to be a fumbling mess. However, that was many years ago now. Before he'd become a marshal. And now he was in charge of all the marshals in the US.

Thankfully, she had never needed his help for anything so serious. Until now. How he would react was anyone's guess. Provided he didn't try to blame Parker for her situation, she was certain, all would be well.

The pair stepped out of the luxurious kitchen, and Parker pointed out his office. It was also in a secure area. This area had been made secure when it was still a saloon, Parker explained. There were multiple bar fights every day and night, and the sheriff was constantly throwing drunks in the cells.

That was when Parker first took over, he told her. He'd closed the saloon down, gutted and revamped the place. Except for changing the name. He'd been unintentionally slow, but it was the next task on his list.

Stepping into the restaurant area took Esther's breath away. It was not merely a restaurant, it was a high class establishment. According to Parker, the restaurant was fully booked every night. Breakfast and lunch were often near capacity, too.

"It is truly beautiful," Esther said. "Your customers must all be rather discerning." Her fingers ran over the stunning hand carved high-backed chairs. Their soft claret red velvet covering the cushioned parts of each chair gave them a cohesive feel. There was also gold beading around the edges, giving it an extra special flair. The tables had matching cloths, and were set to the highest standard.

Esther could see herself working here. Especially in the astonishing kitchen. She glanced up at Parker who hadn't said a word as she touched and assessed the dining room. "This is no saloon," she said gruffly.

Instead of answering, Parker laughed. "You are correct. It took a lot of work, and money, to bring it to this point."

"And yet, it is still called a saloon. Why?" She was incredulous. Although she could see bringing in customers was not an issue.

Again, he laughed. "I can't think of a suitable name for it." He shook his head then, leading Esther to believe he couldn't understand he'd let it hold him back.

"I'm sure you will come up with something suitable." She was certain he would. Eventually. "The kettle should be boiled by now." She turned around Sand was shocked. So much she couldn't speak. Esther lifted a hand and pointed to the window. There stood a man, his face pressed against the large window looking in.

Without warning, Parker held a gun, pointing it toward the stranger. Despite the perceived danger, Esther studied the scene in front of her. "Wait," she demanded, still staring at the man. "I…I think it's Robbie." She ran over to the window and the man pulled back.

"Esther," he shouted. "It's me, Robbie, your big brother." She could barely hear the words he spoke, but zoned in on the man on the other side of the window. It was hard to tell if it was Robbie or not. Just because the man said he was, didn't make it so.

"Star!" he shouted loudly. That was all she needed to know.

Esther sighed with relief.

Chapter Twenty

Parker still held tight to the Colt in his hand. Until Esther could confirm it was indeed her brother, he would not let down his guard. He promised to protect her, and that's exactly what he intended to do.

He moved to the restaurant entrance, and pushed Esther behind him. His heart pounded in anticipation of what may happen, but he still kept a cool head about him. He would prefer to send Esther back to the kitchen, except he needed her to identify if this man was indeed her brother, Robbie. Parker opened the door slightly. Only far enough to see who was outside. A group of men stood awaiting entrance.

"Star," the man shouted. "Let me in."

"It's Robbie," she confirmed, and Parker opened the door wider. As much as Esther wanted to go out and greet her brother, he would not allow her to be seen outside.

"Stay behind me," Parker said firmly as the men all filed inside. Once they were all in, the door was firmly closed and locked.

Esther ran to her brother. "Robbie!" she said, emotion in her voice. "Am I glad to see you." Robbie pulled her close. The pair embraced as though they hadn't seen each other for a very long time. "This is Parker," Esther told Robbie. "He rescued me."

Robbie studied Parker momentarily. This was the part Parker was dreading. "Thank you," Robbie said, shaking Parker's hand. "Words cannot say how very grateful I am." Then his arms were around Esther again.

Moments later, Antoine came running into the restaurant, gun in hand. "What's all the commotion?" he asked, then glanced around the room. "Oh," he said when he spotted the man with his arms around Esther. There was no mistaking they knew and loved each other. "The water is boiled," he said instead, and went back to his kitchen.

Esther laughed. "We'd best go to the kitchen. Who is up for coffee?" Ten pairs of hands shot up, and Parker knew it would be a busy day. Esther led her brother into the kitchen while the others waited in the dining room. Antoine may not welcome so many strangers. He was quite particular about who he allowed there.

"Antoine," Esther said. "This is my brother Robbie." Antoine dried his hands with a kitchen towel, then the two men shook hands. "We have ten extra for coffee," Esther told him. "Point me in the right direction and I'll get it," she told him.

The chef shrugged. "Mademoiselle Chef," he said with a cheeky grin. "I shall make the coffee, if you can finish off the croissants."

Esther's face lit up, as Parker knew it would. She longed to bake, and had been itching to get into Antoine's kitchen almost since she arrived. The two chefs had formed a kinship with each other, which Parker found heart warming. Antoine handed her an apron, and she got straight to work.

"Finally," Robbie said, "I will get to taste your baking."

"Or not," Esther told him. "These are for the breakfast rush."

"It is fine," Antoine told her. "We can make more." His grin told Parker, Antoine was happy to help out.

The smile on Esther's face was priceless. He hadn't seen her so happy before. The combination of having her brother by her side, along with having the use of the kitchen, obviously filled her with joy. Parker watched as she placed each croissant on a tray, ready to go into the oven. She brushed each one with an egg mix, then put the tray aside.

Antoine busied himself with the coffees, then, with Parker following, headed out to the dining room. "Take a seat, my friends," he said. "Breakfast will be forthcoming. As soon it is it out of the oven."

There was a lot of mumbling and plenty of appreciative comments as Antoine placed the coffee on the tables.

One of the marshals approached Parker. "Could you close the blind? It will be safer for everyone that way."

Parker glanced across to the window. "Of course," he said. "I rarely close it because it is usually dark in here until opening time." He strode across the room and did as requested. He also pulled down the blind on the door.

Why he hadn't thought of it before, Parker wasn't sure. Esther's pursuers could have found her through his lack of insight.

He turned around to find the marshal standing behind him. "Don't blame yourself," the marshal said. "You were not to know."

Parker nodded but wasn't sure he agreed. He believed he'd done everything possible to keep Esther safe, but now wondered if it was true.

"Thank you, but I'll only feel better when I know Esther is safe." Parker headed back to the tables in the knowledge no one could see what went on behind the large glass window. He glanced across the tables. Each man appeared weary, which wasn't surprising. "Thank you all for coming," Parker said. "I truly appreciate it, and I know Esther does as well. Breakfast is in the oven," he announced. "Our chef, Antoine, along with our Esther have made something very special."

The men muttered between themselves again, then sat quietly as they drank their coffee. Parker returned to the kitchen where the delicious aroma of freshly baked croissants overtook his senses. "I need to visit you down here more often," he told Antoine.

He glanced across at Esther who smiled as she worked. It was perfectly clear to Parker this was the place that made her the happiest. After all this madness was over, would she go back to Helena and work in the dingy diner that underpaid and underappreciated her?

The mere thought of it broke his heart. If she left Silvercrest, Parker knew he would never see her again.

Chapter Twenty-One

Esther was in her element. Antoine had made perfect pastry for the croissants, as she knew he would. Never had she seen more perfect pastry. It was soft to the touch, and she was certain it would tantalize the taste buds.

That he was willing to give up his hard work for her brother and his marshals made her feel more than a little thankful.

Antoine had done a lot for her. Far more than Esther expected he would. Once she knew about Charlotte, she completely understood. Parker was the same – they might not have been able to help Charlotte, but they could help her.

Esther appreciated it more than they would ever know.

"That's the last tray," she told Antoine when he stepped back into the kitchen. "What do you want me to do next?"

"Whatever your heart desires," he answered, and she couldn't help but grin.

Free run of Antoine's incredible kitchen? She couldn't have anticipated anything better. "Hmmm," she said, thinking out loud. "Danishes?" She studied him in anticipation.

"Of course, mon amie," he told her, then showed Esther where to find the ingredients she needed. "But are you certain you wish to spend the time?"

"I am. It is my way of thanking you and Parker. Along with Robbie and the marshals too," she said, her voice full of emotion.

She watched as Parker took a step toward her, but Robbie was there far quicker. As much as she loved her brother, having Parker's arms around her was special. She saw the disappointment on Parker's face, and threw him a smile. Her heart pounded at the look he gave her. He understood the situation and was happy for her.

Besides, they would be alone later and he could hold her then.

She mixed all the ingredients in the large bowl and reveled in the high quality equipment Antoine had to work with. Never had she been afforded such luxury. The equipment at the diner in Helena, consisted of anything the owner's wife no longer wanted in her kitchen. So basically hand-me-down kitchen supplies. It was depressing, but what could she do? She was facing a losing battle even asking for more appropriate kitchen supplies.

She was filled with warmth as she worked. Esther loved her job, and apart from spending time with those she loved, baking was her second love. She loved the creativity it brought, and loved using her hands to make something incredibly special.

As the last of the croissants came out of the oven, she was almost ready to add the Danishes. All she needed now was for the stewed apples to be cool enough. "Have you made these for your breakfast clientele before?" Esther asked Antoine.

"Never," he said firmly. "They are being spoiled today." The smile on his face told Esther he was not unhappy about the gesture.

With the stewed apples now in place on the pastry bases, Esther placed the lattice over the top of each one and brushed them with the egg wash. She then placed them in the oven.

Her heart was filled with joy. Not only was her brother here, with more than sufficient back up, but she got to do something she truly loved.

"What do you know about Sheriff Dodd?" Robbie asked Parker quietly. But not quietly enough – Esther heard the question, and was curious why he'd even asked.

Parker glanced across at her, and Esther pretended not to hear. She continued with what she was doing. Instead of having the discussion right there in the saloon kitchen, Parker took Robbie aside. The two talked in low tones for several minutes before returning to where they were previously.

"Why don't you join your marshals in the dining room?" Esther asked her brother. "You must be hungry, too."

"I can eat here," Robbie answered, his face full of curiosity.

Esther was about to tell him no, when Antoine intervened. "No eating in my kitchen," he said firmly. "This is where we prepare and cook food and it must be pristine." He waved a hand to indicate the cleanliness of the preparation area. Esther had to admit, it was likely the cleanest kitchen she'd ever worked in.

"Off you go," she told her brother when he turned to face her. "I'm fine here. I have Antoine and Parker to protect me." Her heart skipped a beat at the mere thought of Parker, and how close they'd become. She never wanted to lose him, but he'd shown himself to be reluctant. Did that mean he truly wasn't interested in her?

Esther sighed. Perhaps she could keep baking. Antoine seemed more than happy to have her assistance. Except she didn't know what to do now. What else, if anything, did Antoine need her to create?

"You look lost, mon amie." Antoine's voice startled her.

"I'm wondering what else you would like me to prepare." She wasn't giving him a choice, merely informing him she didn't know what else was required.

He raised his eyebrows, then smiled. "Our breakfast menu is limited. Croissants or bacon and eggs with a side of tomatoes." That was a disappointment. Esther truly wanted to help out. "However, you could work on the desserts for the lunch crowd," he said, mischief written all over his face. "We need Crème Brûlée – about a dozen would do. We also offer Crepe Suzette," he told her. "Of course, these are made fresh as ordered."

"Of course," Esther repeated. Instead of brooding over how limited she was, Esther began work on the Crème Brûlée. They needed to be made early, to ensure they were cold by the time they were needed. She had just finished the custard component and poured them into the fancy dishes Antoine provided, and was about to begin work on the caramel discs when she heard the commotion.

Before she knew what was happening, Antoine had snatched her up and pushed her into the large pantry. Esther knew she was trembling, but couldn't help herself. It was then she realized Parker was missing. Had he wandered out into the dining room with Robbie? She had been so focused on what she was doing, she hadn't seen him leave.

Chapter Twenty-Two

Parker was startled by the pounding on the door.

"It's Sheriff Dodd," the voice called. The sound was somewhat muffled by the glass door, along with the blind Parker had closed earlier.

He glanced at Robbie. "What do you want me to do?"

Rubbing a hand through his hair, it was clear Robbie was concerned. He wasn't certain what do to, that much was clear. He motioned for some of the marshals to come closer. If need be, they would be ready. "Lift the side of the blind carefully. If it's him, tell me. If not, we will deal with it."

"What aren't you telling me?" Parker demanded before opening the blind.

Robbie studied him. "We've had our eye on your sheriff for some time now. He appears to have links to the brothel owner."

"Brutus Ahearn." Parker's words were full of anger. Did Sheriff Dodd cause his sister's abduction? He wanted to…

"Parker! You need to calm down," Robbie said firmly. "I understand, I really do. Check if it's Dodd, and if so, we will handle it."

Anger still filled him, but Parker fought to calm himself down. Then he pulled back the blind ever so slightly. He gave a little wave to the sheriff, then stepped back, allowing Robbie and the marshals to do what they did best.

"Please return to the kitchen, and stay with Esther and Antoine," Robbie said. "Ensure they are safe."

Parker shrugged his shoulders. He knew better than to argue with Robbie, and headed toward the kitchen. Almost the moment he was out of sight, he heard the commotion coming from the dining room. Parker was tempted to return, but was sure he would be more of a hindrance.

His heart shattered when he found the kitchen empty. He took some deep breaths, trying to calm himself. It seemed the morning was one stressful event after another. Except when he watched Esther creating. It was very clear she was in her element.

He glanced around the room. Antoine was not here, and neither was Esther. That could only mean Antoine had taken her to safety. His gaze fell to the large pantry at the back of the room. He hurried to it, at the same time moving quietly. He didn't want to give their position away if that's where they were.

Being ever so quiet, Parker slipped inside the pantry, only to be confronted by a gun wielding man.

"Mon ami!" Antoine whispered. "I thought you were one of the low-life criminals." He lowered his gun and put it away. Parker didn't even know Antoine carried a gun – it wasn't something they had ever discussed. Still, he didn't blame Antoine for doing so. "What is going on?" the chef demanded. "There was quite a ruckus out there."

"It was Sheriff Dodd. Robbie believes the man is dirty, and passing information to the brothel owner."

He heard Esther gasp. "Should we stay here?" she whispered. Even in the near darkness, it was clear she was terrified.

"I believe it's the safest thing to do. Robbie sent me in here to protect you, but Antoine beat me to it."

"You think I would abandon a lady in distress?" Antoine said fiercely. "You blaspheme." If it hadn't been serious, Parker might have laughed. It wasn't really blasphemy, but perhaps it was close.

Suddenly his attention moved from within the pantry to outside of it. Right there in the kitchen, was another commotion. At least it's what he believed. "Stay here," he demanded, then carefully put his head around the corner of the pantry.

"There's no one there," he said, once he'd slithered back into the pantry. "Do not move," he told Esther firmly, while keeping his voice to a whisper.

Robbie had all but demanded he protect Esther, his little sister. It was the only thing Parker was interested in doing at this time, and would ensure her safety. Even if it meant putting himself between a bullet and Esther.

Antoine grabbed Esther by the hand and pushed her underneath a table at the back of the pantry. The infrequently used equipment sat on that table, and it was the perfect hiding spot. Why they didn't think of that before, Parker wasn't sure. Perhaps Antoine thought it unnecessary previously. Everything seemed to change very quickly. It was worrying.

Suddenly, there really was movement in the kitchen, with footsteps getting closer. Both Parker and Antoine held their guns, pointing them toward the pantry entrance. The pair concealed the area where they'd hidden Esther.

"Where is my sister?" Robbie asked, his voice full of emotion. "Was she harmed?" He completely ignored the two guns pointing in his direction.

The two men moved aside, and Esther scurried out of her hiding place. She ran to her brother, whose face was covered in blood, along with his clothing. Parker watched as the two embraced, and knew he would do the same thing in Robbie's position.

"We have arrested *Sheriff Dodd*, along with the criminals he'd brought with him. This is the very reason I decided to drive through the night to get here."

"You're hurt," Esther said, pulling back from her brother.

He brushed her concerns aside. "We are yet to find and arrest Brutus Ahearn," Robbie said. "He is the most dangerous of all. Once we get him, we can ensure the safety of the women being held hostage at his brothel."

"In other words," Parker said with disdain in his voice, "he sent his thugs to do his dirty work."

"Your sheriff amongst them," Robbie added.

Parker had been right all along. Sheriff Dodd was the link to the brothel. He was no doubt telling the brothel owner where to find women. At least now he would be suitably punished, although in Parker's mind, no punishment would be sufficient for what the man had done.

Chapter Twenty-Three

Esther couldn't believe what she was hearing. She thought it was strange the way Sheriff Dodd had behaved in Parker's suite, but simply thought he needed more proof. Instead he was planning a way to hand her back to Brutus Ahearn.

How could a lawman do such a thing? It made her wonder about his deputy, but Robbie hadn't mentioned him at all. She glanced up at Robbie. There was a lot of blood, and it churned her stomach. Not the blood itself, but the fact she'd put him in a power of danger.

Without thinking, she reached up and touched his cheek. There was a large cut, which looked like it may require stitches.

"The blood isn't mine," he said, pulling her hand away. "It's from the thug I have since arrested. As they say, you should see the other guy." He chuckled then, and Esther frowned.

"You have a nasty cut on your cheek. So yes, it is your blood." Even to her own ears, she sounded annoyed. Esther knew she had every right to be.

This was Robbie doing his big brother thing – trying to make her feel better and not worrying about himself.

"I'll get the doc," Parker said, his eyes never leaving her face.

"Not yet," Robbie told him firmly. "We don't know how safe it is out there."

"Provided Esther is in here, she is safe. I'm getting the doc." Parker headed toward the kitchen entrance, and Robbie called out to him.

"Don't go alone," he demanded. "Take at least two of my marshals. You don't know what you'll encounter out there."

Esther knew Robbie was right. She also knew this entire scenario could have been avoided if there were no brothels, and the people running them had some scruples. As it was, they didn't care who they snatched from the streets. Brutus Ahearn was the ring leader and the others were mere lackeys, including Sheriff Dodd. It made Esther wonder how many other lawman were on the brothel owner's payroll.

No matter, it was out of her hands. Her concern right now was her brother's welfare. And Parker's too. She didn't like the thought of him going outside. Who knew what or who he would come up against?

"Star?" Robbie's voice was loud and grinding.

She gazed up at him. "What?" she almost screeched, and realized it was due to stress. She never behaved this way.

He glanced down at her with love in his eyes. The sort of love you expect from your big brother. "I said, I am okay. I have endured far worse." He rubbed a bloody hand through his hair. "We should find somewhere to sit down." He led her to the dining room, but it was pure bedlam. Marshals were spread across the room, and several men, scruffy looking men, were handcuffed.

She studied the prisoners. Esther's heart pounded. "Those two," she said pointing at two specific men. "They are the men who kidnapped me in Helena."

"Let's get the prisoners in the cells," Robbie commanded. "Including the so-called sheriff." The last words were almost a snarl. Esther had never seen Robbie like this, and she was beginning to wish she never did. Still, he was a good lawman, always had been. He would not have been elevated to his position otherwise.

It wasn't long before Parker and the marshals returned with Doc Billings. Esther couldn't believe how much relief she felt.

The doc glanced about, no doubt mentally checking each man for injuries, but went straight to Robbie. "I'll need a bowl of hot water, along with an empty bowl," he requested.

Esther was on her feet and disappeared in no time. In the kitchen, Antoine was taking her Danishes out of the oven. "They are perfect, mon amie," he told her.

In all the commotion, she'd forgotten about them, which was totally understandable. "Thank you, my dear, dear, friend," she said with far too much emotion in her voice. Esther was convinced if she didn't hurry with her task, she might break down, and that would never do.

Antoine hurried across to where she stood. He wrapped his arms around her, and Esther did not complain. A tear rolled down her cheek, and she admonished herself for being so emotional. There was no time for such things. She had to get the requested items out to the doc.

Finally, she came to her senses and pushed away from him. "I have to get some supplies to the doc," she said. It was then she realized she had no idea where to find the bowls. "I need two bowls, one filled with hot water," she said, this time her voice was more stable. Not emotional like before.

Antoine studied her. "Of course, mon amie," he said, then hurried to collect the items. "Why don't you prepare your Danishes, and I'll deliver the bowls to the doc?"

She knew what he was doing. Antoine was trying to keep her away from watching Robbie as he was treated. It was probably for the best. Doc Billings knew what he was doing.

Esther nodded. She stared down into her hands to find them covered in blood. She shouldn't be surprised. Robbie was covered in blood, his own, and perhaps even that of the criminals he'd tackled. The thought cut through to her core.

She hurried over to the sink and scrubbed her hands with hot water and soap, until there wasn't a trace of blood anywhere to be seen. Then she tended to her Danishes. She had enjoyed her time in Antoine's kitchen, but sooner than later, her time here would be over. The mere thought of it left her heart broken.

~*~

Esther stood at the pristine kitchen counter, waiting for word from Robbie. Parker was in the dining room, looking after their breakfast customers. Antoine was by her side.

"Do not stress, mon amie," Antoine told her. "Soon we will find out what happened. For now, we have customers to look after."

Of course he was right. Customers always came first, and it was far too late to cancel the breakfast rush, as much as Parker wanted to do so. Antoine convinced him otherwise.

It had taken all three of them to tidy up the dining room. Chairs had been overturned, but thankfully none were broken. Even the glass window had stayed intact, which was a blessing. Replacing the large window would be more than a little expensive.

Parker hurried into the kitchen. "Passing on accolades from the customers. They are enjoying the croissants and Danishes."

"You offered my Danishes for breakfast?" Esther asked. "They were supposed to be for lunch."

Both men laughed. "What the customers want, they get," Parker said. "I explained there would be Danishes available for lunch today, and some demanded them immediately. How could I refuse?"

Esther agreed. He couldn't deny the request, especially when he told the customers they were already made. "They were a hit. We may have to add them to our regular menu," Parker added. "But only if you are here to make them."

His words confused Esther. "You want me to help Antoine in the kitchen?" Her eyes strayed from Parker to Antoine. The chef was grinning, but Parker was frowning.

"Mon amie," Antoine said gently. "I think he might be asking you…"

He was interrupted by Parker. "I'm asking if you will marry me," he said.

"Rather awkwardly," Antoine added, then chuckled.

"Yes!" Esther told him. She didn't need to think about it, not even for a moment.

Parker embraced her, then pulled away. "I need to get back to the customers, but I won't be much longer," he said, then disappeared.

"Time to make more Danishes?" Esther asked the chef. She would be guided by him.

"There are still enough," Antoine said. "Have you ever made Coconut Cake?" he asked. "It is a classic French dessert."

"I have not," Esther said, disappointed she would be letting him down. In the short time she had worked with Antoine, she had come to see him as a mentor of sorts.

"Then I shall teach you," he said, then set about doing just that.

~*~

It was quiet once the dining room was cleared of customers. The waitress Parker employed was clearing the tables, and wiping them down ready for the lunch rush. At least they got a break in between meal services.

"We are serving chicken crepes for lunch today," Antoine announced.

Esther studied him momentarily. "Do you only serve French cuisine?" she asked.

"It is the difference between this establishment and others. It is what keeps the customers coming. So, oui. We only serve French cuisine."

Esther's head shot up when she heard the front door close. She rushed out to the dining room, then halted when she saw Robbie. He ran to Esther and embraced her. "It's all over," he whispered. "Brutus Ahearn is in jail, along with his associates."

Her heart soared. "And the women he held captive?"

"Freed, every one of them," Robbie told her. "All thanks to you."

It was what she needed to hear.

Epilogue

Five months later…

With the trial over, life could finally get back to normal. Brutus Ahearn and Peter Dodd were both hanged, and the rest of the criminals were jailed for life. They deserved nothing less.

First item on Parker's agenda was to marry Esther, and a week later, that's exactly what he did. The ceremony was a small one, with only family and close friends. It was what they both wanted. Robbie offered to give Esther away, and she jumped at the chance. With both their parents gone, he was her only family, and Esther loved him dearly.

As big brothers went, Robbie was a particularly good one. Before meeting him, Parker was apprehensive regarding how Esther's brother would feel about him. They formed an almost immediate friendship, despite the circumstances, which Parker treasured. It was despite Parker bringing his little sister to his private suite after he'd rescued her.

Antoine decided he too, wanted to be Esther's big brother, keeping an eye out for her when Robbie wasn't around. They all became a tight-knit group, and Parker couldn't be happier.

Next thing on his list was to rename the *saloon*. The time had long passed, and Parker knew it. With everything Robbie had done to help Esther, he'd asked his now brother-in-law to do the honors, unveiling the renaming of the business.

"I now officially declare this establishment the *Star Restaurant*," Robbie said to the large group of people gathered outside for the unveiling. His eyes drifted to his sister, standing beside her husband. The love Robbie had for his sister was clear, and her expression reflected the same. One thing Parker knew – Robbie would always be a big part of their lives. He wouldn't have it any other way.

Nothing had changed inside the restaurant, it didn't need to. The food was, as always incredible, but for now, Antoine had his own sous-chef. Although in truth, he treated Esther as an equal, not an assistant. Her swollen belly was well and truly showing, and as much as she denied it, a few more months and she would need to hang up her apron.

For a while at least.

"Well, Mrs. Gerard," Parker whispered, "you appear exhausted. "Perhaps a nap is in order?"

"And miss the party? Not on your life!" she said, clearly exasperated. Parker couldn't help but hear Antoine's laughter. He was supposed to be on Parker's side.

Still, he knew Antoine was enjoying having Esther's expertise in the kitchen. It was no longer *his* kitchen, but *theirs*.

It had been good for Antoine. Before Esther was helping him, Antoine worked alone. Now, he would even take a day off, which he never did before.

"What delicacies did you and Antoine conjure up for the renaming party?" Parker wondered out loud.

Esther smiled. "Wouldn't you like to know," she said as she tried to contain her laughter.

"You are so cruel," Parker said jokingly, and pulled Esther tighter still.

As everyone headed inside, Parker held back, holding Esther in his arms. "I love you more each day," he whispered, not prepared to let others hear his words meant only for his wife. "You are a cherished part of my life," he told her.

"And you are precious to me, too," Esther told him. "Without you, my heart would be empty. I truly love you, Parker," she whispered.

They waited until everyone was inside before entering. That is when they saw it – Antoine was chatting with one of the townsfolk. If he wasn't mistaken, it was Amelia from the inn. With his arm around her, Antoine led her to one of the tables, and ensured she was comfortable.

Parker's heart was full of joy. Not only because he'd married Esther, but also because Antoine had finally opened his heart after losing their dear Charlotte.

From the Author

Thank you so much for reading my book – I hope you enjoyed it.

I would greatly appreciate you leaving a review where you purchased, even if it is only a one-liner. It helps to have my books more visible!

About the Author

Multi-published, award-winning and bestselling author Cheryl Wright, former secretary, debt collector, account manager, writing coach, and shopping tour hostess, loves reading.

She writes historical romantic suspense and historical western romance.

She lives in Melbourne, Australia, and is married with two adult children and has six grandchildren, and twin great-grandchildren.

When she's not writing, she can be found in her craft room making greeting cards.

Links

Website: *http://www.cheryl-wright.com/*

Facebook Reader Group:
https://www.facebook.com/groups/cherylwrightauthor/

Join My Newsletter:

https://cheryl-wright.com/newsletter/
(and receive a free book)